N7P

D1758402

B

A CASE FOR DR. MORELLE

There are few cases of Dr. Morelle, the famous criminal investigator, where his secretary Miss Frayle doesn't come to the forefront of the picture. Indeed, eminent friends of the Doctor's have said that Miss Frayle was in some respects the most important part of the Doctor's criminological equipment. It was the murder of her erstwhile employer that had introduced Miss Frayle to the Doctor, and murder was to become a recurring link in their uneasy relationship . . .

ERNEST DUDLEY

◆

A
CASE FOR
DR. MORELLE

Complete and Unabridged

LINFORD
Leicester

First published in Great Britain

First Linford Edition
published 2010

British Library CIP Data

Dudley, Ernest.
  A case for Dr. Morelle. - -
  (Linford mystery library)
  1. Morelle, Doctor (Fictitious character)- -
  Fiction. 2. Private investigators- -Fiction.
  3. Secretaries- -Fiction. 4. Murder- -Fiction.
  5. Detective and mystery stories.
  6. Large type books.
  I. Title II. Series
  823.9'14–dc22

  ISBN 978–1–44480–028–9

Published by
F. A. Thorpe (Publishing)
Anstey, Leicestershire

Set by Words & Graphics Ltd.
Anstey, Leicestershire
Printed and bound in Great Britain by
T. J. International Ltd., Padstow, Cornwall

1

Dr. Morelle Finds a Secretary

Entry in Doctor Morelle's personal diary, dated March 5th, year not indicated:

'Today a young woman answering to name of Miss Frayle entered my employ. I fear my inherent good nature persuaded me to offer her the post of assistant in my research and laboratory activities and act as secretary. She would appear to suffer from an astigmatic condition of the vision and wears spectacles that do little to enhance her somewhat unprepossessing appearance. However, she appears to be a willing worker and possesses a self-effacing personality. Whether these characteristics are the result of low intelligence and moronic mentality I am not certain. I fear it to be the case. No doubt the young woman will shortly commence to presume upon my generosity and grow inefficient — or by her timorousness and anxiety to please irritate me beyond endurance. In any event it would appear I shall not be long before having to dispense with her services, and my magnanimous gesture will be finally discharged.'

★ ★ ★

It was at a late hour one moonless and rather misty night when Doctor Morelle was proceeding somewhat briskly along Chelsea Embankment. He had just left the house of Sir Burton Muir, the eminent K.C., and a small party of friends with whom he had been dining. It had been a pleasurable evening, good food excellently cooked and served, good wine; together with a flow of conversation befitting the intellect of guests and host. Doctor Morelle had as was his habit made brilliant contribution to each various topic of discussion scoring points with his sardonic shafts of humour. He had left before the others, having in mind some work awaiting him unfinished in his laboratory. Now having decided to take a little exercise before ultimately hailing a taxi he was walking quickly along the embankment in the direction of Chelsea Bridge.

Somewhere down river a ship's siren hooted mournfully and the Thames running past was dark and forbidding. The mist swirled chill and raw across the Embankment, which seemed quite deserted. But as he strode on, his mind full of the research problems with which he presently proposed to grapple, Doctor Morelle passed the figure of a young woman leaning against the parapet. He might not have noticed her so insignificant a figure she made, but something, a certain tenseness about her attitude caused him to throw her a passing glance. A few paces on he paused to light a cigarette. As he flicked a flame against the tip of his Egyptian Le Sphinx he glanced back, and snapping the cap of his lighter into place swiftly retraced his steps.

'You know,' he said to her, and his tone was level and charged with a sardonic quirk, 'I don't think you should!'

She gave a startled gasp. 'Oh . . . ' His swift and noiseless approach had taken her utterly unawares. He regarded her.

She was small and slim, pathetic in her shabby clothes, and she stared up at him wide-eyed through horn-rimmed spectacles that were perched awry on her nose. The look of desperation in her face gave way now to one of forlorn misery and wretchedness.

'Drowning is a cold and dismal affair only a fool would choose,' he murmured.

'I'm not going to — ' Her attempted denial faded into a broken whisper, and she turned away to stare down at the dark waters. Unmoved he watched the tear-trickle run down her nose and splash onto the parapet. He said:

'I can suggest several other ways of committing suicide, much more pleasant.' He paused as if to decide for her which method might prove most acceptable. Then he sighed, and with a tone of disappointment, added: 'Regrettably, however, it would be wrong of me to name them.'

'Please — please leave me alone . . . '

He had no intention of acceding to her request until his curiosity had been satisfied. Insinuatingly he said: 'Should I

— er — call a policeman?'

Her face jerked up to him in terror. 'No! Oh, don't!'

'Very well. But in return you must tell me something. Who are you?'

She said hesitantly: 'My name is Frayle — Miss Frayle.'

'And what — Miss Frayle — ' and now he smiled thinly, 'apart from contemplating putting an end to your life — do you do?'

'I'm — ' she corrected herself with a little shudder, 'I was a secretary-companion.'

'Your employer I presume having dispensed with your services?'

The reply was a whisper he only just caught. 'She's dead.'

'Oh . . . ?' he queried after a brief pause. She began to dab her face with her handkerchief and blow her nose. Now she spoke hurriedly, blurting out the words as if anxious to get rid of them: 'I went out just now to post the letters — I do every evening — and when I came back found her . . . ' Her voice rose hysterically. 'I didn't do it! I didn't — !'

He cut in quickly, deceptively soft-voiced.

'What happened then?'

'I — I lost my head . . . The way she looked! Oh, it was horrible!' She shuddered violently, her face contorted at the remembered horror. 'I rushed from the flat.'

'Without waiting to call a doctor — or inform the police?'

She heard the coldness in his tone, and burst out: 'I daren't! You don't understand. They'll say I did it — she was always telling people — her friends — once even the hall-porter — I hated her, I wanted to see her dead — ' she broke off, and then added pathetically, 'She wasn't very nice sometimes. She was — '

Again he cut in. 'Supposing, Miss Frayle,' he suggested, 'you and I go back to the flat together?'

'Oh, no!' she gasped, terrified. 'I can't — I couldn't face it — !'

He surveyed the glowing tip of his cigarette. Without looking at her, without raising his voice: 'I think it would be better for you if you did as I say.'

Her reaction to the implied threat

behind the quietly spoken words was almost violent. 'No, no — !'

She might not have spoken, Doctor Morelle glanced at the mist swirling about them, gave a somewhat over elaborate shiver and added: 'Besides, I am finding it a little chilly.'

'I won't go back — !' Her voice rose stubbornly. 'You can't make me — ' She broke off with a strangled gasp as a bulky figure loomed up suddenly and a deep cockney voice obtruded itself.

'Here, here — now — ' said the newcomer paternally.

'Ah, good evening, officer,' Doctor Morelle greeted him imperturbably.

'Anything the matter?' the policeman inquired, scowling slightly at Miss Frayle as if to imply that it must be she and obviously not the other who was responsible if anything was untoward. Miss Frayle tried to melt behind the Doctor. 'Er — nothing — it's nothing — ' she murmured.

'Lot o' noise about nothink!' observed the policeman agreeably and gave Doctor Morelle the benefit of half a grin.

'Perhaps I may explain. I am a doctor,

this young lady is my patient, and she is somewhat hysterical. A nervous case, you understand, officer?'

The officer nodded with fullest understanding. He had a daughter of his own, 'difficult' young woman she was. Worry of her mother's life. 'Oh . . . ' he said. 'I see.' And nodded more vigorously.

'I'm just about to conduct her home.' And to Miss Frayle in that insinuating tone: 'Am I not, Miss Frayle?'

There was only one answer she knew. Knew also that he realised she knew. She glanced up at his saturnine face shadowed by his soft black hat. Out of the tail of her eye she caught the glint of official buttons and trembled. After all, she told herself, the other had said he was a doctor. Perhaps he really was. She tried to reassure herself but with sinking heart had to admit he was like no other doctor she had ever met. Nothing kindly and gentle about him. This tall and gaunt, almost sinister figure with the sardonic smile and penetrating, mesmeric eyes.

'Yes . . . Yes . . . ' she answered him in a whisper. 'We'll go now.'

The policeman grunted approvingly and Doctor Morelle observed in an undertone: 'I thought you'd be sensible!' He raised his voice and said briskly, 'Now come along . . . ' And taking her arm pressed it as an indication she was to lead the way. Involuntarily she obeyed and turned towards the direction from which he had come when he had first passed her. As they moved off together, the police officer called out heartily: 'Goodnight, sir.'

The Doctor condescended to throw him a brief 'goodnight' over his shoulder.

Several minutes later they arrived at the front entrance to Bankside Mansions. It was a typical block of flats of the smaller type, with a short flight of steps running up from the pavement to the doorway. The double doors were still open and Doctor Morelle paused at the entrance to survey the small foyer beyond.

'Here we are,' said Miss Frayle unnecessarily.

'The porter is still on duty.' He turned to her. 'Did he see you come out?'

'No . . . I used the back stairs, not the lift. We're only on the second floor.' They

9

had spoken in low tones, for the porter whom Doctor Morelle had observed was standing by the lift-gates expectantly awaiting their approach. They went in.

''Ello, Miss Frayle?' the porter greeted her cheerily, but with a note of slight surprise. 'Good evenin', sir.' He was an undersized, sandy-haired man, aged about forty-five. He wore a dark uniform, but no cap. There was a cigarette-stub peeping from behind one ear. As they stepped into the lift Miss Frayle made a forlorn attempt to brighten up.

'Good evening,' she said, but her smile was unconvincing.

'You looks a bit done-in, Miss,' commiserated the porter, clanging the lift-gates together and pressing the button. The lift whirred upwards.

'The young lady was taken ill in the street,' said Doctor Morelle.

'Oh, dear,' exclaimed the other sadly, shifting his gaze from Miss Frayle and staring at her companion. After a pause during which the Doctor gazed abstractedly into space, the man said: 'I didn't notice yer go out, Miss.'

She began to answer him, stammering to find a non-committal explanation, but Doctor Morelle covered her confused fluttering, asking slowly: 'You've been on duty here all evening, have you?'

'S'right. I'm just goin' orf now. My missus sometimes gets them attacks,' with a nod towards Miss Frayle. 'Verdegris, the doctor calls it . . . Second floor!'

The lift stopped, the gates opened and they stepped out.

'Well, I 'opes yer'll be better in the morning, Miss.'

'Thank you.'

'Mr. Dacre ain't arrived yet,' he went on, as he closed the gates after him. 'Expect he will presently. Goodnight,' and he disappeared from view.

Doctor Morelle turned to her. 'Who is Mr. Dacre?'

'Her nephew. She was Miss Dacre,' she explained. Her face lit up slightly. 'He's very kind.' She frowned. 'I'd forgotten he's expected tonight. Oh, it'll be awful for him — '

'And you lived with her alone? Except when he came?'

'Yes.'

They stood in front of a door painted pale green with a chromium number on it. She refrained from saying: 'This is the flat' — somewhat to his disappointment — instead produced a key and turned it in the Yale lock. He followed her into the small hall, closing the door behind him. She went on ahead of him, while he stood and gazed round with apparent disinterest. On his right was a miniature hallstand holding a woman's overcoat, hat and umbrella. Beyond it a door, closed; another door beyond that, slightly ajar. On his left was a large window, then a passage, probably leading to the kitchen and bathroom; past that another door, closed. The floor was carpeted; there were two or three prints on the walls and a bowl of flowers in a corner.

'You left the light on,' he said.

She was about to enter the room directly in front of her, the door of which was half-open. She turned and said apologetically: 'I know. I must have forgotten when I rushed out.'

He took off his hat, placed it on a chair,

with his walking stick alongside and his gloves. 'This — this is her room,' she whispered. 'I — I must have left the light on here, too.'

He moved towards where she stood, irresolute. If he noticed her face was white and that she was visibly trembling he gave no sign. 'She always locked her bedroom door when she went to bed.'

'What was she afraid of?'

'Her jewellery. She kept it in her room.'

'The door is half-open now. Was it like that when you came back after posting the letters?'

She nodded. 'The light wasn't on.'

'You have already explained you must have omitted to switch it off when you made your precipitate exit.'

Again she nodded dumbly. Then moaned: 'I — I can't go in again.'

'You must. Follow me.' He preceded her into the bedroom. He stood at the foot of the bed for a moment, then moved swiftly round to Miss Dacre. She was dead and her end had been a violent one. A brief, cursory examination was all that was necessary to show she had been smothered to death. He stood up, lit a cigarette. Behind him a weak, shaky voice said: 'Oh, it's too horrible.'

Without giving her a glance he snapped:

'Then sit down and look the other way.'

Feeling sick and faint Miss Frayle obeyed. It seemed to him apparent a pillow had been used to suffocate the woman; he was about to bend to examine one that was disarranged from the others when something soft and warm brushed against his leg. With an exclamation of slight surprise he glanced down.

'What — ? Whose cat?'

'Miss Dacre's.' She called to the animal, purring loudly now. 'Pharaoh, come here?'

A flicker of amusement showed on Doctor Morelle's lips. 'Pharaoh?'

'She believed cats were the reincarnation of Egyptian gods,' Miss Frayle explained.

'He has a very dark complexion for an Egyptian!' was his dry comment. Suddenly he stooped to examine something on the floor. He did not touch the object, but noted it had fallen as if dropped from the dead woman's left hand, which drooped over the side of the bed.

'That's her lorgnette,' offered Miss Frayle helpfully as she stroked the cat now curled at her feet.

'I had already surmised that myself,' he replied. He went on, half-aloud: 'The cord's broken as if wrenched from her neck.'

'You mean, there was a struggle?'

'No doubt your deduction might be correct!'

A thrill of excitement momentarily replaced her trepidation and apprehension. He added without a glimmer of amusement in his face: 'Would you not care to wrap the exhibit in my handkerchief?'

Her spectacles nearly slipped off her nose as she hastened to obey his suggestion. If she heard it she did not heed the sardonic note in his voice as he murmured: 'Carefully, in case there may be some fingerprints on it! Now, place it on that table.'

She could hardly speak with excitement. 'You — you think it might be a cl-clue?' she stammered.

'Not for one moment! Merely that you seem to attach such importance to it!'

Her face fell. 'Oh . . . Well, perhaps I'd better sit down again and mind Pharaoh.'

'That might prove of some positive assistance, Miss Frayle. Or perhaps you could — ?' He broke off. 'Just a moment,' he said and crossed the room. 'The window is slightly open, I perceive.'

'That's unusual . . . She always kept it closed at night.'

'Unhygienic!' he remarked, opening the window wider and peering out. 'It leads to the fire escape. It would have been a relatively simple matter for someone to force the catch and enter and exit this way.'

'You mean the murderer?'

'He would hardly have called in merely to say 'goodnight'! I wonder if her jewellery has been removed — ? No matter for the moment.' He gazed round the room abstractedly as he moved over to her. 'You say she always locked herself in at night? Wouldn't she open the door to anyone?'

'Only sometimes to her nephew. He looked after her business interests. If he came in late from the City when he was staying here she'd want to talk to him perhaps about business.'

'I gather Miss Dacre was a woman of means?'

'She was well-off, yes. But — but rather mean.'

He fixed his eyes upon her. With a chill running down her spine she saw that his pupils perceptibly expanded and contracted. They gripped her with an almost sinister fascination, so that she was compelled to rivet her gaze on his. After a moment, when she felt sure she was about to succumb to a mesmeric trance, his eyelids flickered down and he turned his head to knock the long ash from his cigarette.

'You didn't like her very much, did you?' he murmured without looking at her. She drew a deep breath to steady her voice.

'I didn't,' she said quietly. 'But I wouldn't — wouldn't have done that.'

He replaced the cigarette between his lips and expelled a spiral of smoke ceilingwards. 'I should like to question the hall porter.'

'I'll get him.'

'That was what I was about to request,' he said. 'However, you have anticipated my wish.' He gave her a bleak smile that seemed to her quite terrifying. 'I'll go now,' she said quickly.

He called after her: 'Place the cat in another room. See it does not contrive to escape.'

The hall-porter when he arrived accompanied by Miss Frayle was suitably impressed with the horror of the tragedy. He had changed the jacket of his uniform for a worn sports coat, and had removed his collar and tie. He mumbled an apology for his appearance, explaining he was preparing for bed when Miss Frayle had called him. 'Poor lady, wot a terrible thing to have happened,' was his comment when acquainted with the circumstances of Mrs. Dacre's death. He seemed sincerely affected. 'One of the nicest tenants we have — er — ' he corrected himself self-consciously ' — had.'

Doctor Morelle's gaze rested on a spot somewhere above the other's head. Nevertheless he had not failed to register the man's pallor and a nerve that

18

twitched at the corner of his right eye. He was trembling slightly, too.

'Before we call the police,' he said, 'perhaps you might care to answer one or two questions?'

'Er — well, there ain't much I can say. You see — '

'You look somewhat shaken.'

'Well, I — '

'It must be an awful shock for you,' Miss Frayle put in sympathetically, and then catching the Doctor's chill look upon her, realised her temerity in speaking and fell into abashed silence. The porter glanced at the bed — the body had been covered by a sheet by Doctor Morelle — and nodded glumly.

'Yes, it is,' he said.

'Doubtless it is an unnerving experience. Partake of a cigarette, it will help to restore your equilibrium.' And the Doctor extended his thin gold cigarette case.

Gingerly the other took a Le Sphinx. 'Oh, thank yer, sir — er — Doctor.' And: 'Oh, thanks ever so,' as Doctor Morelle held out his lighter.

'Now . . . tell me, you have been on

19

duty all this evening, I seem to recollect you declaring?'

'Since teatime.'

'Can you also recollect what persons used the lift while you were in charge of it?'

'There wasn't very many.' He pondered for a moment. 'Let's see . . . It was just after I come on I took Miss Jarrow up to her flat on the third. About five o'clock that'd be . . . Then half an hour later, I suppose, I brings Mr. and Mrs. Farrell down from the fourth . . . Little arter six I took Mr. Riley up to three — he was visitin' Mr. Woodham, tenant of the flat there, often does . . . And then . . . ' He paused, scratching his head.

'It would appear no one unknown to you made use of the lift?'

'No.' The answer was definite.

'How about the stairs?' Miss Frayle said. 'Mightn't somebody have — '

The Doctor's voice was like a whiplash. 'I am not incapable of conducting my own interrogation, Miss Frayle.'

She mumbled an apology, blushing and fiddling with her spectacles. The porter

20

coughed in a sympathetic effort to cover up her embarrassment, and eyed his cigarette. 'Posh cigarettes, these, all right,' he said. 'Don't often smoke one like this,' and tried a half-grin to relieve the tension. All of which was lost on Doctor Morelle, who was not even aware either of them had said anything.

'You took Miss Frayle down when she went out to the post?' he pursued.

''S'right. About ten that was.'

The Doctor did not condescend to glance at her for corroboration of this. The other went on: 'Out about fifteen minutes she was, then I brings her back up here again. 'S'right, ain't it, Miss?'

Miss Frayle nodded mutely.

'The — er, ah — stairs?'

'I tell yer nobody could've used them without me seeing 'em. Even the times I'm in the lift I keeps me peepers peeled. Been one or two burglaries round these parts, lately there have, so I — '

'You seem positive no one could have visited any of the flats, and this one in particular, without your cognisance?'

'Eh?' The man gaped at him without

understanding for a moment. Then it sank in. 'No,' he declared. 'No one could have, and that's a fact. Stake me life.'

'I imagine the lift may be operated by remote control?'

'Oh, yes. So if me or the other porter 'appens to be orf for the moment, anyone wantin' it can call the lift and work it theirselves. But we're usually around when the bell rings.'

'And the porter who was on duty before you?'

The other laughed confidently. 'He wouldn't let no one up without arskin' 'em their business. More'n his job's worth. No. I'm no deteckertive, but it strikes me somebody from one o' the flats must have done the pore lady in.' He tapped the ash off his cigarette with an aggressively knowing air. Doctor Morelle regarded the grey ash in the ashtray momentarily and then eyed the cigarette, which the other had returned to his mouth.

'I think we may count ourselves fortunate that you are *not* a — ' he paused almost imperceptibly to emphasise the correct pronunciation ' — detective!'

The man shifted uncomfortably. As if there was a somewhat unpleasant odour offending his sensitively chiselled nose, the Doctor turned away from him and addressed Miss Frayle: 'During your brief absence just now,' he said, 'I took the opportunity of ascertaining that there is a tradesman's entrance from the kitchen. It opens onto the iron staircase which connects also with the fire escape.' He inclined his head to the window and then regarded her unblinkingly.

She stared at him uneasily. Was he waiting for her to speak, she asked herself, fidgetting nervously with the collar of her dress. She decided perhaps he was expecting her to say something. 'Yes — that — that's quite right,' she stammered, and then stopped, awaiting his cold rebuke.

'I am gratified to learn,' he murmured sardonically, 'that you are not entirely devoid of your power to articulate!'

Miserably, Miss Frayle looked at him through her spectacles. Whatever she said or left unsaid, did or did not do, it was bound it seemed to be wrong so far as he was concerned. The first glimmerings of a realisation that there was nothing she could do about this state of affairs began to break in on her consciousness. She could not know she was in fact establishing a basis for a philosophy upon which she was in future to rely.

He was speaking again. She strove to concentrate upon what he said. Her desire to please him was so obvious it would have been pathetic — to anyone but Doctor Morelle.

'I ascertained furthermore,' he was saying, 'that the kitchen door opening onto the iron staircase was locked and bolted on the inside.' He paused to draw at his cigarette and slowly expelled the smoke. 'What,' he queried, 'does that convey to you?'

She goggled at him helplessly. 'To — to me?' she said. He nodded. She creased her brow. 'The door was locked and bolted on the inside,' she repeated slowly. 'I — I'm sorry, but I can't see anything special in that. It always was locked and bolted at night.'

'Quite right, too,' put in the porter.

'Unless,' she went on hopefully, 'it means that no one could have got into the flat that way while I was out?'

He rewarded her with fleeting quirk of his thin lips. 'Precisely, my dear Miss Frayle,' he said. But she couldn't decide whether his over-emphasised term of affection was meant in a kindly way or as sheer sarcasm. She concluded it must be the latter.

'I can't see as it could mean more'n that, neither,' the other man volunteered.

'Your opinion was not solicited,' came the instant rejoinder and at that moment they heard a faint humming sound.

'Someone usin' the lift,' explained the porter at once.

'It's probably Mr. Dacre!' she exclaimed.

'Ar,' said the man and made as if to move to the bedroom door.

Doctor Morelle shot a glance at Miss Frayle's agitated face and snapped: 'You think so?' then to the other: 'Remain here!'

'Why? Wot — ?'

'Do as I instruct you!'

'Here, wot the blazes — ?' The man's

tone was truculent, though he stood irresolutely staring at the Doctor.

'In point of fact,' was snapped back at him, 'you will find yourself unable to do otherwise! The cigarette you have been smoking contains a narcotic which completely paralyses the nether limbs.'

The porter gulped, speechless, terror-stricken. Beads of perspiration glistened on his face. He stood as if rooted to the spot. Doctor Morelle turned to Miss Frayle, who stood with mouth agape: 'Quick! Bring my walking stick. Close the front door. Switch off the hall light and return here. Move — !'

Miss Frayle shot out of the room as if from a catapult and was back in an instant. The whine of the lift grew louder. He took his walking stick from her without a word and motioned her to one side. As the lift jerked to a stop and they heard the gates slide open, he switched off the light and swiftly but quietly closed the bedroom door. They were in darkness. The sound of the porter's laboured, puzzled breathing was broken by Miss Frayle gasping: 'Doctor! What — what are you going to — ?'

'Sssh! Quiet! Not a sound from either of you!'

She subsided, and the porter who was about to protest against such swift and unexpected happenings, groaned and was also silent. There was a moment's pause, then the sound of a key turning in the Yale lock. Miss Frayle shivered with apprehension. Perhaps it was not her nice Mr. Dacre, after all. Perhaps it was — she hardly dare allow the idea take shape — perhaps it was the murderer, returning to the scene of his crime. A phrase she had once read came back to her, ill-remembered, but something to the effect that murderers always return to the scene of their dark deed.

The front door opened and closed. Footsteps approached, then a voice called out: 'Miss Frayle . . . ' It was nice Mr. Dacre after all. She relaxed with a little smile and drew a breath to call out to him, when a hand was clamped over her mouth. Doctor Morelle's voice hissed in her ear: 'Keep quiet! *Don't answer!*'

Again the newcomer's pleasant voice

was heard: 'Miss Frayle! Are you there?'

There was a slight pause as if he was making sure there was no reply, then the bedroom door opened and the light snapped on.

'What — ?' Dacre began, staring first at Doctor Morelle, who stood leaning negligently on his walking stick, then at the porter, who tried to grin that he wasn't at all responsible for such proceedings.

'Mr. Dacre — ' stammered Miss Frayle as his gaze rested on her, But that was as far as she got, for the Doctor's soft: 'Good evening,' swung his eyes back to him. He was a tallish, pleasant-faced young man, frowning now and non-plussed. Suddenly he saw the shape on the bed, and a quick glance at their faces brought from him a gasp of inquiry:

'Oh . . . What — what's happened?'

With a quick movement he was at the bedside. 'Oohh — !' A great cry of distress and shocked, broken tones: 'The poor thing — ! Oh . . . the poor thing — !'

'This must be a terrible shock to you, I

know — ' Doctor Morelle said quietly.

Dacre shot a look up at him, a penetrating glance, and his voice was belligerent. 'Who are you?'

Miss Frayle began: 'Mr. Dacre, I — I — if you'll let me explain — '

The Doctor brushed her aside. 'I am Doctor Morelle,' he said with great dignity, great simplicity. 'Miss Frayle — er — called me in.'

'Oh . . . ' Dacre gestured towards the bed. 'When did this — this happen?'

'Death occurred between forty and fifty minutes ago . . . As a result of suffocation.' He glanced down suddenly as something warm and soft brushed against his legs. He fixed a cold stare on Miss Frayle. 'I thought I instructed you — ?' he began, but she broke in.

'I'm so sorry. I — I couldn't have closed the door properly on him. I'm so sorry . . . ' She called to the cat. 'Pharaoh, come here — ' Purring loudly the animal walked slowly over to her.

Doctor Morelle turned to Dacre. 'The facts in this — er — unfortunate tragedy may be elucidated quite simply.' He spoke slowly, enjoying the full flavour of the attention that was now riveted on him. He paused and calmly swept their faces with his gaze until again he was speaking to the young man. He allowed a faintly derisive smile to play about the corner of his mouth, and taking a Le Sphinx from his cigarette case, lighting it, said:

'But I feel sure, Mr. Dacre, you would not wish to be bored by my recapitulation of those facts?'

Miss Frayle noticed his grasp of the walking stick tightened as Dacre took a pace forward, his jaw set. 'What the devil d'you mean?' he demanded.

Without taking his eyes off him, the Doctor spoke to the porter:

'Go into the sitting room,' he said, 'and telephone the police . . . It is all right, you will be able to move now, the effects of the narcotic have worn off.'

Muttering the man started for the door.

'Keep back — !' Doctor Morelle rapped out the words as Dacre lunged forward at the porter. As he spoke there was a scrape of steel and the blade flashed from his walking stick, its point at the young man's chest. Dacre stepped back, his face suddenly haggard and grey, a wild, trapped look on it.

'Blimey! A swordstick!' exclaimed the porter and dived into another room where he could be heard urgently telephoning Scotland Yard.

There was a moan and a thud behind Doctor Morelle as Miss Frayle collapsed in a dead faint. Doctor Morelle, however, did not take his eyes off the dangerous figure he held pinned in the corner. Somehow he seemed to convey the impression that even had he been able with safety to turn his head, he would hardly have bothered to do so.

★ ★ ★

Doctor Morelle lit his Le Sphinx and said:

'Waiting outside the flats until the moment he saw Miss Frayle go out to the post, Dacre slipped, by way of the tradesman's entrance, up the iron staircase. He entered the flat by the kitchen window, which he had carefully studied and learned how with the aid of a thin, strong penknife he could contrive to open it from the outside. By knocking at his aunt's bedroom door in the usual way he was by that unsuspecting woman admitted.'

He was addressing his elucidation of Miss Dacre's murder to the Divisional Inspector. They were in the sitting room of the flat. Dacre had been removed, after breaking down and confessing to the crime. In the bedroom the police-surgeon had made his examination; and photographers and fingerprint experts were completing their work. Miss Frayle, somewhat recovered from her faintness but bemused and terribly tired, sat listening to Doctor Morelle, trying hard to take in what he was saying. The Divisional Inspector raised an expectant eyebrow and the Doctor proceeded:

'After Dacre had smothered her with the aid of the pillow, he took the jewels — the motive for his crime — and made his exit through the bedroom window, deliberately leaving it open to create the impression the murder was an outside affair. He had closed the kitchen window behind him. Unfortunately for him, however, he committed one error.'

He paused again, this time to heighten to the full the dramatic effect of his next words. The Divisional Inspector however took this opportunity to observe sententiously: 'They always do!'

The Doctor eyed him coldly. 'He omitted to lock the bedroom door behind him,' he went on, an ill-tempered note in his voice, 'and gave away damning knowledge of his error when he returned later. For . . . thinking Miss Frayle to be absent he walked directly into his aunt's room, *without pause to knock or even test whether it was locked*. Had Dacre been innocent of any knowledge of his aunt's death he would certainly, believing her to be alive, have gone through his habitual procedure before entering the room.'

He allowed himself a sardonic smile of triumph as the Divisional Inspector stared at him in open admiration.

'By God, that was smart of you!' the other exclaimed. 'Damned smart!'

Doctor Morelle gave a slight shrug and

knocked the ash off his Le Sphinx.

Miss Frayle said: 'I still don't understand about that drugged cigarette you gave the porter . . . '

He spread his hands in an indulgent gesture. 'The cigarette was, of course, perfectly innocuous, I fear I was prevaricating when I informed him it was a paralysing drug. I merely wished to prevent him from revealing to Dacre that we were in the flat.'

She said:

'But it did paralyse him — he couldn't move a step!'

'Merely auto-suggestion, my dear Miss Frayle. His will-power is considerably under-developed, and I found him a singularly easy subject on whom to demonstrate the — er — shall we say — peculiar gifts I happen to possess!' And with wonderfully assumed casualness Doctor Morelle crushed the stub of his cigarette into the ashtray.

2

The Somnambulist's Secret

Miss Frayle glanced briefly at her diary, was about to close it when her eyes widened behind her spectacles, her mouth made an 'O' of incredulity, She glanced again at the page and made a rapid mental calculation. It was true, she had been with him a year. With a long sigh, she leant back in her chair and stared out of the window.

Her thoughts retraced themselves over the past months. It seemed ages ago — and yet it might have been only yesterday — when she first met him.

Anyway it had been a year unique in her experience. Unique, she told herself, in the experience of any young woman. A year she was not likely to forget. Moreover she was beginning to arrive at the uncomfortable conviction that the year beginning and each one succeeding, it would be equally strenuous, hectic and disturbing. Equally nightmarish.

Doctor Morelle was like that. His magnetic personality not only attracted all with those he came into contact (while it simultaneously repelled some). It also attracted Trouble. Miss Frayle spelt it in her mind with a capital 'T' because it wasn't ordinary trouble. Not at all the kind she had associated with a doctor's practice, such as awkward patients, urgent midnight telephone calls and so on. Nothing like that about *him*! No, it was always Trouble that was queer and sinister.

Like that business about the Grey Parrot. With anyone else it would have been psittacosis or something. Not very nice for the poor parrot and upsetting for its owners, of course. But when the Doctor was investigating the Grey Parrot affair it turned out to be much worse than anything like that. She repressed a shudder as she thought about it. A horrid, fantastic business. She had nightmares about it still.

She supposed she was being rather unjust to the Doctor. He wasn't really the cause for awful things happening, it was silly to pretend he was. But if only he wasn't so interested in anything unusual, so — she searched her mind for the word — so bizarre. That was it. If only he would just deal with ordinary cases the same as any other Harley Street doctor. She got up and went to a shelf of books that chanced to catch her eye,

The titles alone were enough to frighten one. In German, French and Italian, with words like *Kriminalanthropologie und kriminalistik; Medecine Legale, Technique Policiere, Criminalle*, and so on . . . The walls of the study were lined with books devoted to such subjects; there were filing cabinets crammed with information on the same theme. The Doctor had one bookcase that ran from floor to ceiling locked, and on an occasion when she had asked the reason for this precaution, his reply had sent chills down her spine. Once or twice a morbid curiosity had prompted her to glance at the thick dossiers ranged behind the glass, but they bore only index numbers for titles. She often thought they really contained nothing frightening at all, and the Doctor's answer to her question about them had simply been another example of his twisted, sardonic sense of humour. All the same even if she did happen to possess the key she wouldn't have opened the bookcase for a thousand pounds.

The telephone broke into Miss Frayle's dubious speculation on the contents of a thick volume bearing a long and sinister sounding title in Spanish.

'Hello . . . This is Doctor Morelle's House. Yes. Oh, yes. Ten-forty tonight at the hospital. I'll tell the Doctor, and will you please convey his thanks to Sir Andrew? Thank you so much. Goodbye.'

She replaced the receiver and made a note in the diary. It was an invitation from Sir Andrew Ridley, the eminent brain specialist, for Doctor Morelle to witness an operation that night. It was an invitation he had been awaiting for the past few days, for the operation was in the nature of an experiment, a new drug being used in connection with it. It was the drug and its effects in which the Doctor was particularly interested. He had been a pioneer in the research work upon it. As a result of his exhaustive study and experiments he and Ridley both felt that a revolutionary discovery had been made which would be of inestimable value in the case of certain more delicate brain operations. Ridley was most enthusiastic about the possibilities of the Doctor's new-found preparation, and was determined to put it into practice upon the first opportunity. That opportunity had now arisen and the surgeon had sent a message asking that Doctor Morelle should be present.

As Miss Frayle scribbled the note the study suddenly darkened and she glanced up to see the sky above the houses opposite was overcast. In a moment there came a gust of wind and a spatter of rain drove against the windows. She frowned and then hurried along to the laboratory where Doctor Morelle was engaged upon some other research work, this time in connection with the final stages of a blood-test experiment. She wanted to inform him of Sir Andrew's news, while there were a number of other appointments of which to remind him. Apart from these an empty inner sensation proclaimed to her the not unimportant fact that it was approaching lunchtime Doctor Morelle was however destined not to be present at the operation to which he had been invited, nor was he to witness the completely successful response of the drug he had discovered to the test to which it was subjected. This disappointment was perhaps counter-balanced by an exciting if somewhat sinister chain of incidents that were set in motion at about the time he should have been setting off for the hospital.

The rain had continued all day and rattled now with unabated fury against the curtained windows. Miss Frayle stood at the study door, holding it open with one hand, while with the other buttoning the top of her raincoat. She gave an anxious look at the figure bent over the mass of papers on the wide desk, apparently oblivious of her presence. Hesitatingly she drew a deep breath and stammered:

'Doctor Morelle — '

'What is it — what *is* it?' he snapped

without raising his head.

'You — you're due at the hospital at ten-forty, and it's gone ten-fifteen already.'

He looked up at once, his expression almost sinister in the glow of the desk-lamp. He turned to the clock in front of him, 'Ten sixteen! And the operation scheduled for ten-forty . . . Why was I not informed it was so late?'

Rising, he thrust the papers to one side with a gesture of irritation and eyed her accusingly. 'Do not stand there goggling at me, answer my question!' She opened her mouth to explain that was the fourth time she had reminded him in the last fifteen minutes of his appointment, but knew she might as well save her breath.

'And might you not agree,' he went on relentlessly, 'that if you removed that agonised expression of self-abnegation from your face and obtained a taxi, it would facilitate my arrival at the hospital?'

'I'll see if I can find one cruising past.'

'Thank you,' he replied sardonically. Then in a tone of self-commiseration: 'As you have omitted to bring my coat and hat I will procure them for myself.' Miss

Frayle gave him a look and hurried away. Returning a few minutes later she found him waiting, tall and dominating in a long overcoat, his walking stick under his arm.

'I've got a taxi,' she said with breathless triumph. 'It's outside the door.'

'I did not imagine you had prevailed upon the driver to bring it into the hall,' he said.

'I was lucky to get it, a night like this. It's still raining.'

He surveyed her glistening coat with over-elaborate surprise. 'Really?' he murmured. 'I was fully under the impression you had been spraying yourself with a watering can of the horticultural variety!' Pulling on his gloves he snapped, 'Come along! I have something more important to do than listen to your obvious ineptitudes.'

She followed his gaunt figure, closing the front door behind them. They stood on the step and bent to the rain-gusts, The taxi-man opened the door and the Doctor motioned her to get in while he gave the address. As he was about to direct the driver, Miss Frayle gave a piercing scream and backed agitatedly out of the taxi, stumbling and half-falling onto the pavement.

'Oh — ! Oh, Doctor Morelle — !'

He caught her arm and prevented her from collapsing altogether. She was moaning now hysterically. 'Good heavens! What is it — ?' he snapped.

The taxi-man lurched across in his seat and said hoarsely. 'Blimey — Wot's up?'

She managed to gasp: 'In — In there! Something — a — a — body!'

'Body?'

'Body — ' echoed the driver, nearly falling out of his seat in astonishment. 'Body, did she say? Oo's — ?'

'Oh!' moaned Miss Frayle. 'I — I touched its face — ' She shuddered with horror.

'Switch on a light, driver.'

'Yes, Guv'nor.' The man obeyed and clambering down, came round to join them. 'Must be seein' things.' He started to grumble, then broke off with a grunt. 'Blimey — ' he exclaimed, 'she *ain't*!'

Eyes narrowed the Doctor regarded the interior of the taxi and remarked: 'If you wish to faint, Miss Frayle, do so elsewhere. One inanimate form is sufficient for the moment.' She reeled to the luggage space beside the driver's seat and sat there, her head between her knees. The rain trickled down the back of her neck.

'Wheeeyew!' whistled the taxi-man through his teeth. 'Dead all right by the looks of him!'

'Hmm . . . Paperknife driven into his heart.'

'Messy sight, ain't it? All that blood on his evening shirt — lucky none of it's got on my floor. But how the devil did he get into my cab?'

'The answer to that question remains to be ascertained. If, meanwhile, you would assist me to carry him into my house.'

'Yes sir,' The man, still puzzling, pushed his cap back and scratched his bald head. 'Yer see,' he went on in explanation, 'you were first fare I 'ad ternight, since I left me rank.'

'Open the front door, Miss Frayle,' the Doctor called, snapping her into action.

'Come on, come on!'

She stood up, shivering as the rain ran half way down her back and as if in a trance obeyed. The driver said, 'Shall I take the feet, Guv'nor, and you 'is head?' Together they carried the body within, the rain beating at them. They placed the dead man in the consulting room.

A little later Doctor Morelle, having concluded his examination came into the study and placed the paperknife, wrapped carefully in a handkerchief, on his desk. Miss Frayle stared at it in fascinated horror. She and the driver had been waiting for the Doctor, and the taxi-man now sat up and cocked an inquiring eye.

'Pulled it out, did yer?'

Doctor Morelle made no reply, but thoughtfully lit an inevitable Le Sphinx. After a moment he said: 'Your surmise then, driver, is that while you left your vehicle, which was alone, on the rank —?'

'Just popped into the pub round the corner, I did.'

'Someone — the murderer, or murderers, presumably, must have deposited the body — '

'That's right, bunged it in me taxi. Blimey, bit of a sauce, eh, Miss?' He turned to Miss Frayle who was blinking at them through her spectacles. Doctor Morelle contrived to curb his impatience with the man's garrulity. He proceeded smoothly, 'All forms of identification have been carefully removed from the deceased. Nothing in his pockets offers any clue. One thing, however, I did observe — '

'I noticed that while his clothes were slightly damp, the soles of his shoes aren't a bit wet or muddy — was that what you were going to say, Doctor?' It was Miss Frayle who somewhat recovered from the shock she had suffered now made the interruption, taking the words out his mouth.

'I *do* wish you would mind your own business!' he snapped at her. '*I* am supposed to — '

'Crikey!' suddenly exclaimed the taxi-driver, banging his cap on his knee, 'that's it! I remember now — '

'What,' asked Doctor Morelle irritably, 'have you recollected?'

'I seen that bloke afore! That scar on

his cheek . . . Yes, that's right! Blimey! Why 'e come out of an 'ouse opposite my rank, and I took him down to the City.'

Miss Frayle gave a squeak of excitement. 'A house by your rank?'

'S'right. Coupler days ago. It was that scar wot reminded me.'

'In which case it might facilitate his identification if you drove me there forthwith,' the Doctor observed.

'Okay.'

'Come along, Miss Frayle . . .'

The rain had slackened to a drizzle when they drew up outside a medium-sized house standing back slightly from the road. A narrow strip of garden on either side isolated it from the other houses, and two or three trees and high shrubbery helped to screen it from passers-by. Opposite as the driver had said was a taxicab rank in the middle of the wide road. The rank was deserted. Miss Frayle and Doctor Morelle stepped out of the taxi, and after he had said something in an undertone to the driver, they both made their way to the front door. The wind soughed in the trees and the rain dripped mournfully against the dark, untidy foliage.

Suddenly the Doctor paused abruptly. He had caught a movement at the ground floor window, the flash of a man's face, white against the darkness. Then the curtain had been quickly drawn again. Miss Frayle, meanwhile, noticing nothing ascended the steps and pressed the bell. She turned as he joined her.

'Have you rung?' he said.

Unable to resist the chance of getting a little of her own back, she answered: 'Oh no, Doctor! I guessed whoever's at home must be psychic!'

'Then perhaps you might care to ring again,' he said with elaborate politeness. She rang twice, long shrilling rings whose echoes within came back to them. There was no reply. Doctor Morelle tapped his stick on the edge of a step, his eyes narrowed speculatively. After a moment he stepped down and crossed to the window. The window at which the mysterious face had appeared. He gave it a brief survey and quickly raised himself onto the wide sill two or three feet from the ground. He took a narrow torch from an inside pocket. It was an ordinary type window, the upper and lower frames secured in the middle by a catch. The light from his torch enabled him to examine it through the glass and he gave an exclamation of satisfaction. He eased the blade of a thin penknife along the centre join. After a moment's pressure there was a sharp click as the catch sprang back.

'What are you doing, Doctor?' Miss Frayle stood below, looking up at him, eyes wide behind her spectacles. He gave her a sardonic glance, pressed against the lower half of the window and as it squeaked upwards, said: 'Effecting an entrance by way of this window, my *dear* Miss Frayle.'

'Oh, but we can't go in that way! Someone might see us! A policeman, or — '

'What a timorous creature! Very well, you remain behind and whistle if danger approaches!'

'The house seems very dark and quiet. Perhaps the taxi-driver was mistaken, or

— not telling the truth. Anyway there seems to be nobody here.'

He merely looked back in the direction of the road. The sound of the taxi-engine ticking over could be heard. He smiled enigmatically and said, 'Are you accompanying me or remaining behind?'

'I — er — I suppose I'd better come with you.'

'I warn you — ' he began darkly.

'I know,' she said quickly. 'There may be trouble. All the same I'll feel safer with you, and anyway I'm tired of the rain trickling down the back of my neck! . . . I can't whistle either!'

'Let us enter,' he said, holding out his hand. She grasped it and stood beside him. 'Follow me.' And pushing the curtain aside, he landed lightly in the room. A moment later and she half fell in, banging her head on the window and bringing from him an unsympathetic chuckle.

'It's awfully dark.'

'A moment and I will ascertain the whereabouts of the light-switch.' A door showed up black against the lighter coloured wall, and he moved over to it unerringly.

'You must have eyes like a cat!' she said.

They were in a well-furnished room, and moved noiselessly on a thick, richly purple carpet. She blinked in the sudden strong light and a fresh wave of panic and doubt assailed her. 'Suppose the police *do* catch us?'

'I imagined you had considered that before you joined me on this burglarious exploit!'

'But it's your fault. You told me to — '

He silenced her protest with a warning wave of the hand and silently opened the door. She followed him into the wide hall. He switched on the light. In the heavy silence that lay over the house, a grandfather clock was ticking away somewhere. It sounded abnormally loud.

'Everything's so quiet,' she breathed.

'Still as a tomb!' He said it deliberately to frighten her. He felt her gasp convulsively and clutch at his arm. With a sardonic smile he turned to her. She was staring, eyes like saucers at something ahead of her. He followed her gaze. At the top of the staircase leading down into the hall stood a figure.

'What — what — ?' gurgled Miss Frayle incoherently.

'Do control yourself,' he snapped irritably.

'Coming downstairs — Doctor, look!'

'A somewhat curious apparition.'

'It's — it's a woman — !'

'Attired one might suppose in a not unbecoming negligee!'

'She looks so strange . . . her eyes — !'

'Hmm . . . A remarkable example of somnambulism. Keep quiet.'

Miss Frayle gulped and clutched his arm more tightly. 'You — you mean she's walking in her sleep?'

'Precisely, Miss Frayle. Watch . . . She is descending as if with some definite purpose.'

'What shall we do if she comes this way?'

They were talking in whispers. Now the woman reached the foot of the stairs and seemed to be about to approach them. Miss Frayle hardly breathed the question.

Suddenly the woman stopped and turned slowly.

'She is proceeding across the hall.'

They watched her move slowly but purposefully towards a door. On reaching it she stopped then opened it and went in. There came the click of the switch as she snapped on the electric light.

'Oughtn't we to do something?' asked Miss Frayle anxiously.

'Wait here a moment. Possibly the creature will be coming this way again.'

She shuddered. 'It's so creepy!'

'Ssh — ! Here she comes now . . . '

'Still sleepwalking.'

'Going back upstairs. No doubt returning to her room . . . There she goes.'

'It's uncanny.'

The woman reached the top of the staircase and disappeared from view.

'She's left the door open,' said Miss Frayle, pointing to the shaft of light that came from the room the sleepwalker had just left.

'We might investigate now and ascertain what, if anything, it was attracted her there,' said the Doctor. 'Come along.'

She followed him and stood just behind him as he paused in the doorway. It was a small library, also used as a study as the heavy, carved desk at one end showed. It was this that at once caught Miss Frayle's attention.

'Look!' she gasped. 'Sitting there — !'

Doctor Morelle crossed the room. 'Hmm . . . curious attitude,' he murmured. 'I fear we shall never wake *him*.'

Miss Frayle stared at the inert figure slumped over the desk, a bullet-wound in his temple. Drops of blood had run down onto his evening shirt. 'He's dead,' she whispered and suddenly felt violently sick. 'Oh!' she moaned, 'I think I'm going to faint — !'

'Do not be so foolish!' he snapped irritably. 'Sit down — put your head between your knees.' She managed to reach a chair and fell into it, then proceeded to follow his advice. She felt terrible. 'This is no time for hysterics,' she heard him saying, as if from far-off, his voice cold as ice. Then he was murmuring to himself, 'Obviously self-inflicted . . . Death must have occurred only a short while ago . . . '

He found the revolver beside the dead man's chair, where it had fallen from his hand. He was about to pick it up for a closer examination, when Miss Frayle gave a gasp of alarm and a man in butler's attire stood in the doorway. His heavy face wore a scowl of interrogation.

'What are you doing here?' he demanded belligerently, coming towards them. He stopped with a horrified look as he saw the figure at the desk. 'Colonel Mason — ! What — what's happened?' he choked.

Doctor Morelle said, 'I am afraid he is dead.'

'But — but — ? What — ?' The man's shocked dismay was painful to watch. 'Oh this is terrible — '

'He has been shot, as you perceive.'

'Murdered — ?'

The Doctor gave him a quick look. 'Why should you imagine it is a case of suicide — ?'

'I — I don't know. I — I — what else could it be — ?'

'It might be an accident. It might be *felo-de-se*. As it happens it is the latter.'

'Suicide?'

'That conclusion is compatible with the evidence before me.'

The butler's gaze travelled from the Doctor to Miss Frayle and back to the Doctor again. 'How — how did you get in here?' he said at last.

Doctor Morelle glanced up casually from the writing-desk and regarded him coolly. 'I believe someone here wishes to see me,' he murmured after an almost imperceptible pause. 'I am Doctor Morelle.' He took a Le Sphinx from his cigarette-case and tapped it carefully. Miss Frayle goggled at him. She was utterly at sea. He inclined his head towards the hall. 'As you would no doubt observe if you went into the other room our mode of ingress was somewhat unconventional. Miss Frayle did, however, ring your bell several times — without effect.'

'I — er — I — Colonel Mason never told me he was sending for a doctor,' he muttered.

'Could it be someone else requires my aid?'

'There's Mr. Lovell,' was the uneasy reply. 'But he's out.'

'How about the lady?' murmured the Doctor through a cloud of cigarette smoke.

The man's uneasiness grew. 'Mrs. Mason? Oh — er — she's asleep.'

'I see.'

At that moment a voice raised inquiringly was heard from the hall: 'Who's there? Is that you, Markham — ?'

The owner of the voice came in. He was a middle-aged man of medium height. He wore a double-breasted evening jacket with a carnation making a crimson splotch on his lapel. He stopped as if he had received a blow.

'Good God — ! Colonel Mason — !' He came forward with a hoarse cry.

'The Colonel's dead, sir,' said the butler. The other was trembling violently. He turned and demanded: 'Who are you? What are you doing here — and this young woman — ?'

'I am Doctor Morelle. Here at the — er — invitation of Mr. Lovell, I believe. This is my assistant, Miss Frayle.'

'When did Mr. Lovell ask you here?'

'About twenty minutes ago.' He turned

blandly to Miss Frayle. 'You *weren't* quite sure of the name, were you?'

She gulped, then stammered: 'Er — no, I wasn't, was I?'

'Though you did say, if you recall,' he insinuated, 'it was a name like Lovell, did you not?'

Her head was reeling, but she contrived to say mechanically. 'Oh, yes; Lovell, or Novell, or Govell — something like that. It was rather difficult to catch over the 'phone.'

'And you found Colonel Mason — like this when you arrived?'

'Precisely.'

'Oh . . .'

'Says it's suicide, sir,' put in the butler.

'Suicide? But — ' The man broke off and stared at the inert figure. He passed his hand in bewilderment over his brow. 'I'm his secretary,' he said jerkily. 'My name's Dale . . . This is terrible. Terrible. You're — you're sure it's suicide?'

'I have no doubt at all.'

'I'm afraid I don't understand about Mr. Lovell,' the other said dazedly. 'Mr. Lovell does live here — he's Colonel

Mason's cousin — but he went out for a luncheon appointment and hasn't returned.' He said to the butler: 'Mr. Lovell's *not* come in, has he, Markham?'

Doctor Morelle caught a fleeting look exchanged between the two men before the other replied: 'No, sir.'

Dale said: 'So I fail to see — er — Doctor, why he should have telephoned you to call here.'

'Might he not have telephoned on Mrs. Mason's behalf?' asked the Doctor quietly, and observed the flicker of uneasiness that appeared in Dale's eyes.

'Mrs. Mason isn't ill. She's asleep. Besides even if she was suddenly in need of a doctor, how could he know if he hasn't been back?'

Doctor Morelle conceded that point with an inclination of his head. But his eyes were narrowed as he abstractedly tapped the tip of his cigarette. He said: 'Mrs. Mason is a victim of somnambulism, is she not?'

Dale started. 'You saw her?'

'She came in here before we did.'

'She was walking in her sleep,' Miss

Frayle said unnecessarily.

The secretary gave a groan of dismay. 'This is unbearable — !'

'Should I tell Mrs. Mason, sir — ?' The butler hesitated, then went on. 'Perhaps it would be better if — '

'No, no! Don't disturb her yet.'

'Very good, sir.'

'I'll ring if I want you, Markham.'

'Er — yes, sir.' The man made to go, then paused. 'Shall I close the window m the other room?'

'What?'

'The window, sir, I — er — I believe it's open. I — er — I didn't hear the Doctor ring, and so they came in by way of it.'

Dale glanced sharply at Doctor Morelle, who however seemed to consider any further explanation unnecessary.

'Close it, Markham. Close it, of course!'

'Yes, sir.'

'Oh . . . '

'Yes, sir — ?'

'If Mr. Lovell should return before the Doctor — ah — goes, let him know he is here.'

'Very good, sir.' There was a further exchange of looks between them and the butler closed the door after him. There was a moment's pause. Then Dale said slowly: 'Doctor, there's something I'd like to ask you . . . Do you believe Mrs. Mason did this — while she was sleepwalking?'

Doctor Morelle regarded him. 'I have already intimated to you,' he said, 'that her husband died from a self-inflicted wound.'

'I know. I was wondering if you really believed that — or if you thought — '

'Apart from the other evidence which I have taken into account, Miss Frayle and I were in the immediate vicinity when in her somnambulistic state Mrs. Mason entered this room. We can both vouch for the fact that we heard no sound of any shot fired.'

Miss Frayle looked at him suddenly. 'Of course!' she exclaimed. 'That proves the poor woman couldn't have done it!'

'Thank you, Miss Frayle!' observed Doctor Morelle with a sardonic smile. He said to the other: 'Your question does, however, raise a not insignificant point.'

'Yes?' Anxiously.

'Why do you imagine Mrs. Mason should wish to murder her husband?'

There was a deathly silence. Then: 'He made her life a hell!'

Doctor Morelle raised his eyebrows a fraction.

Dale went on: 'Are you going to fetch the police?'

'I fear that will be necessary.'

'*You won't* . . . ' came the grim answer, and with a sudden movement the man bent and picked up the revolver. Miss Frayle gave a squeal of fright. 'Oh — !'

The Doctor eyed the white, twisted face behind the gun. 'Calm yourself, now!' he murmured.

'Don't move, either of you, and put up your hands!' Miss Frayle raised hers with such alacrity that she knocked her spectacles off. She stood there, blinking shortsightedly, too terrified to retrieve them. 'Come on, Doctor Who-ever-you-are! Put your hands up!'

'The name is Morelle — Doctor Morelle — and your attitude will not help matters — '

'If you don't raise your hands, I fire!'

'Perhaps I should point out that I am something of an expert on firearms, and that the one you are holding now happens to be unloaded.'

'What — ?' Dale crumpled, his mouth gaping stupidly. Doctor Morelle smiled thinly.

'If you will just place it on the desk? Thank you. And Miss Frayle, you may return your spectacles to their appropriate place now.'

'Thank you, Doctor — '

'Anyone might imagine,' Doctor Morelle said smoothly, 'that you were in love with Mrs. Mason . . . And not as I surmise to be the case, the absent Mr. Lovell.'

Dale stared at him like a man seeing a ghost. 'How — how did you know?' he said in a low voice.

'That Mr. Lovell was enamoured of Mrs. Mason?'

The other nodded.

The Doctor glanced at his watch. His ear caught the sound of what might have been a taxi-engine fading away into the distance and an enigmatic expression

63

flickered across his face. 'By the way,' he said, 'I wonder what is delaying him?'

'Mr. Lovell?'

'Mr. Lovell.'

'Yes . . . ' Dale licked his lips nervously. 'I expected him back before this. Probably the rain may have held him up or something.'

Miss Frayle glanced quickly at Doctor Morelle. He seemed to be engrossed in a picture on the wall immediately behind the desk. She said brightly: 'It's been raining all day . . . Hasn't it?' But they were paying no attention and her voice trailed off.

Suddenly the Doctor stepped forward. 'Is this a photograph of Mr. Lovell?' he asked. 'In flannels and blazer?'

Dale glanced at the wall and nodded. 'But how did you guess? You've never seen him before, have you?'

Doctor Morelle gave him a non-committal look. Without turning his head, he said: 'You recognise him, Miss Frayle, do you not?'

'Except that the scar doesn't show,' she answered, after a moment's scrutiny.

'No . . . the scar is not visible. Is it, Mr. Dale?'

'Umm? Oh, the scar? No, it wouldn't show in that picture.' He frowned uneasily and was about to say something more when the door opened. It was the butler again.

'Did you ring, sir?' he asked, and Miss Frayle sensed a sinister purposefulness in the manner in which he closed the door. Trembling apprehensively she glanced at the Doctor. Somewhat to her surprise he was fixing the butler with a sardonic grin.

He said: 'It would appear your hearing is more acute when one does not ring for you, than when one does!'

The man made no reply, but turned questioningly to Dale. Doctor Morelle said: 'However, since you seem anxious to be of some service, I suggest you find a covering to place over the deceased until the police arrive.'

The man looked at Dale again, who nodded. 'Yes . . . do that, Markham. It will look better . . . ' The butler went out. The Doctor had turned his attention to a black metal contraption beside the writing desk.

'Colonel Mason's dictaphone,' said Dale.

'I perceive it has an attachment by which one may hear what has been spoken onto the cylinder . . . It might be interesting to listen.'

The other said nothing. Doctor Morelle pressed the device that operated the machine. The cylinder started to revolve, and in a moment a voice, slightly distorted by the mechanism, could be heard:

'*Friday evening . . .* ' said the voice. '*Reminder to make appointment with Gresham tomorrow . . .* ' There was a pause. Then: '*Reminder to ask Dale to go into details of North Western Railway shares . . .* '

'Can you hear, Miss Frayle?' asked the Doctor in the next pause.

'It's uncanny,' she whispered.

The voice again: '*Reminder to tell Dale to obtain documents relating to Fletcher and Morgan Company . . .* '

'That is Colonel Mason's voice?'

queried Doctor Morelle.

Dale nodded. 'Yes. He must have been using it this evening; making notes for some business he planned to work on tomorrow.'

'I had somehow imagined that to be the case,' the Doctor replied smoothly.

'A — a voice from the grave . . . ' Miss Frayle said. She stared at the dictaphone and shivered.

'A somewhat melodramatic observation, not to say morbid!' Doctor Morelle said. The voice had stopped. All that could be heard was the scratch of the needle on the revolving cylinder. Doctor Morelle stopped the machine. 'I would prefer you to exercise your imagination more profitably,' he went on. 'What for example have you deduced from this little exhibition of mechanical ingenuity?'

Miss Frayle's face was a blank. 'Wh — what?' she stammered.

'I might have known!' was his only comment, and he turned to Dale.

'I'm afraid I don't see that it proves anything,' he said, with a puzzled frown.

'Does not the fact that Colonel Mason

was this evening making plans in a normal way for tomorrow postulate that he did not anticipate his approaching demise?'

'Why, yes.'

'Precisely. At what time would you say did he use the dictaphone tonight?'

'Oh, before dinner. He never worked later than that.'

'We have to ascertain therefore what it was caused him to take his life during the two or three hours after he had quitted this room to change and dine. Yes?'

'I — I suppose so . . . Yes.'

The butler re-entered and placed a sheet over the dead man. Miss Frayle looked away, feeling sick again. Somehow she felt the figure looked more gruesome now than it had appeared before. She noticed with a sudden apprehension that the butler after completing his task closed the door and stood as if guarding it. Doctor Morelle, however, appeared to be unaware of the man's presence. His attention seemed attracted to the writing desk. Suddenly he moved to it and picked up an envelope from two or three others stacked against a heavy inkstand.

'Curious,' he murmured abstractedly. 'This envelope, like the others here, would seem to have been opened with the aid of a paperknife. And yet,' he paused studiously to run an eye over the desk, 'no implement for that purpose would seem to be evident.'

Neither Dale nor the other spoke. Doctor Morelle raised a saturnine face and went on coolly: 'It would also appear from the cut edges of the envelope that the — er — absent paperknife was — shall we say — an adequately sharp instrument . . . '

'Put the damned letter down!' Dale exclaimed thickly. 'What's it got to do with Colonel Mason's death?'

'I was not at that moment thinking of Colonel Mason,' said the Doctor softly. At that moment the doorbell rang.

'Who the devil — ?' began Dale, and Doctor Morelle murmured: 'Possibly Mr. Lovell has returned, and has forgotten his key?' He added, with a glance at the butler, who had already made as if to answer the ring: 'I am gratified to note

69

that your hearing has become normal!'

The bell rang again. 'Go and see who it is, Markham!'

'Yes, sir.'

In a moment he was back, followed by a police-sergeant and a constable. In the background hovered the taxi-driver.

''Ere we are, sir!' he grinned cheerily at the Doctor. 'Gave yer fifteen minutes like yer said, then went and fetched the cops — !' He coughed with mock embarrassment, winked at the two police-men and corrected himself. 'Sorry! *Perlice*, I should've said!'

While Miss Frayle blinked unbeliev-ingly at the new arrivals, and the butler stood indecisively looking from one to the other, Dale made an attempt at bluster. 'What the blazes is the idea?' he barked. The police-sergeant, who had been staring at the white shape by the desk, turned to Doctor Morelle. He was negligently tapping a shoe with the end of his walking stick. He raised his eyes as the sergeant began to speak and anticipated the question.

'Your inquiries will no doubt begin,

officer, with Colonel Mason's suicide and the circumstances surrounding it. I should like to point out, however, that this unfortunate tragedy is inter-related with the death of Colonel Mason's cousin, a Mr. Lovell, whose body at this moment reposes in my consulting room.'

'The man's mad!' exclaimed Dale, his face twisted with rage and fury. 'Mad, I tell you — !'

Breathless, goggling at the scene, Miss Frayle caught a movement from the butler, as he stepped forward aggressively. The constable, however, motioned him back, and the man checked himself. The taxi-driver who had now obtained a clear view of the sheet-draped figure, blurted out: 'Blimey! Another body . . . 'Ow many more of 'em!'

Imperturbably — he might have been dictating a letter to her, Miss Frayle thought — the Doctor proceeded, 'Therefore, officer, pursuing your inquiries you will in due course find it necessary to question Mr. Dale here as to what knowledge he has regarding the murder of the aforementioned Mr. Lovell. In the event of a not unnatural desire on his part to evade some of your more leading questions, I feel confident I am in a position to furnish all the relative answers — '

'I tell you my cousin hasn't come back yet!' Dale's voice rose. 'He went out to lunch, and — '

'In his evening clothes,' queried Doctor Morelle through a cloud of cigarette smoke. He smiled thinly as the other's jaw sagged. 'That was the apparel he was wearing when found in the taxi — '

'S'right!' put in the driver.

'When therefore you declared he had not returned home from his luncheon appointment I knew you were prevaricating — you had obviously instructed your butler to assist in the deception. Conceding the possibility, remote though it might be, that Mr. Lovell had returned, changed his clothes and gone out again without either of you being aware of the fact, it would have been impossible,' his voice was raised a fraction in emphasis, 'for him to have quitted the house of his own volition without his shoes becoming wet and muddy in the rain!' He paused to savour the dramatic effect his words had upon them. The silence was electric. He went on: 'The conclusion to be inferred was obvious. He must have been carried out of the house.'

He blew a spiral of smoke ceilingwards. 'We come now to the late Colonel Mason,' he went on, 'and the connection between his and Mr. Lovell's demise. The evidence supporting my theory that Colonel Mason committed *felo-de-se* — '

'Suicide?' said the police-sergeant.

'Precisely . . . The evidence is irrefutable. We next ask ourselves why he took his own life. He is a man of fifty years of age or so, of some means,' he indicated the surroundings with a wave of his walking stick, 'and still actively engaged in business. His secretary, Mr. Dale, cannot advance the suggestion that financial difficulties or business anxieties drove him to death.'

He paused for Dale to speak. The man remained silent.

'But his attitude did suggest the fear that Mrs. Mason might in fact have murdered her husband. What prompted that fear? I postulate that Mrs. Mason's affections were, or were about to be, transferred elsewhere. To whom? Why not Mr. Lovell? As you may ascertain from that photograph he was a not unhandsome man. Someone also nearer Mrs. Mason's age. She as most of us here are aware is young, attractive no doubt. Of a somewhat neurotic temperament she revealed the secret she shared with Lovell to her husband — probably spoke the other man's name during one of her somnambulistic states. Tonight Colonel Mason charged Lovell with alienating his wife's affections. Bitter words were exchanged. A blow was struck. A body was removed and deposited in an empty taxi across the way — '

'S'right,' said the driver.

'Remorse overtook Colonel Mason,' went on Doctor Morelle, inexorably, 'remorse and fear of the consequences . . . ' He indicated the white figure. 'The rest you know. No doubt Mr. Dale will in due course acquaint you with the facts as to who assisted in the disposal of the body — he or the butler — '

At that moment Dale rushed the door. The constable stopped him, however, with a neat punch to the jaw, and almost with the same movement snapped the handcuffs on him.

'Accessory after the fact,' the sergeant said heavily. The taxi-driver who was enjoying the situation enormously had edged himself towards the writing desk. Eyes popping with curiosity he picked up the revolver Doctor Morelle had placed there. The Doctor saw the action and rapped out a warning:

'Put that revolver down!'

But the driver had squeezed the trigger. There was a loud report and a hole appeared in the ceiling.

'Blimey!' exclaimed the taxi-man dropping the gun as if it were a hot brick. The sergeant picked it up quickly.

'Here, here!' he said censoriously. 'Better let me take care o' that, before you shoot someone!'

Miss Frayle was staring open-mouthed at Doctor Morelle.

'But — but you said it was unloaded,' she stammered.

He surveyed her sardonically. 'Did I?' he queried. 'Dear me! I fear I must have been bluffing . . . '

Came a long drawn out sigh from Miss Frayle, and she slumped to the floor in a dead faint. Doctor Morelle regarded her with a slight frown, examined the tip of his Le Sphinx and said to the taxi-driver: 'I think you had better take us home.' And he stubbed out the cigarette.

3

The Chemist in the Cupboard

'Quickly — the acid, Miss Frayle!'

Miss Frayle rapidly scanned the row of test tubes and bottles.

'The small phial — next to the iron sulphate — ' snapped Doctor Morelle, his hand outstretched impatiently.

His peremptory command flustered her for a moment. She snatched the phial and caught it against a large container of distilled water. There was a crash and tinkling of broken glass. Without a word and with incredible quickness the Doctor took Miss Frayle's hand and placed it under the full force of the cold water tap. Then he examined it carefully.

'You are singularly fortunate. You might have sustained a very nasty burn.'

Miss Frayle readjusted her glasses and regained her breath.

'I — I'm sorry, Doctor Morelle,' she

managed to stammer. 'It slipped and — '

'I am not incapable of perceiving you do not appear to exercise full control over your digital extremities! Has the acid splashed your clothes at all?'

'No — just the corner of my overall.'

He seized a bottle of alkaline solution and applied it liberally to the part of her overall indicated. Then he turned out the Bunsen burner beneath the retort that had been emitting a pungent odour.

'That brings our little experiment to an abrupt conclusion for the time being at any rate,' he said with a chilling glance at her.

'I'm so sorry, Doctor,' she apologised again.

'I think your expressions of regret might well take a practical form, Miss Frayle. Perhaps you would care to procure another phial of acid for me.'

'If you'll tell me the name — '

'I'll write it down. It's just possible that Mr. Jordan may be of some assistance to me. You know his shop?'

'The little chemist's shop in the turning off Welbeck Street? Will there be anyone there at this time?'

'Mr. Jordan resides on the establishment. You will ring at the side entrance. I have written the formula on this card of mine — you will present it to Mr. Jordan with my compliments.'

She took the card upon which he had scribbled his requirements. He went on.

'I am confident he will have a sufficient supply to enable me to carry on with my work tonight. So that if you will hasten, Miss Frayle, I should have time in which to complete the experiment I am engaged upon before retiring for the night.'

Miss Frayle hurried off, while Doctor Morelle lit an inevitable Le Sphinx cigarette and then divested himself of his white coat. In a moment he had returned to his study to make some notes.

Despite its undistinguished frontage, Miss Frayle had no difficulty in finding Mr. Jordan's chemist shop. She made her way to the side door that was in a narrow entrance between the shop and a garage. She rang three times, but there was no response. No sound of any movement within. She knocked loudly. It was then she realised that the door was not firmly fastened. Her first knock sent it slightly ajar. She banged the old iron knocker again, but there was still no reply. After a pause she stepped inside with some idea of perhaps finding Mr. Jordan in a room at the back. A strong smell of antiseptics greeted her as she hesitated for some moments, trying to make up her mind whether to call out or not.

She called quietly at first: 'Mr. Jordan?' Then louder. But no reply.

At the far end of the tiny hallway, she noticed a flight of stairs. Thinking the chemist might be occupied in an upstairs room and perhaps slightly deaf, she decided she had better investigate further. It was a choice between that and going back without the precious acid. She decided she could not face the sardonic rebuffs from Doctor Morelle if she should return empty-handed.

Very gingerly, she began to climb the stairs. It was only a short flight, opening on to a small landing which was crowded with crates, packing cases and cardboard boxes of all descriptions. She tapped on the door immediately facing her, and as there was no reply, tried the handle, feeling more and more like a person intent upon some guilty purpose.

The door opened to reveal an unusual-looking room. It was a combination of warehouse, laboratory, office and living room. Nearest the door were still more packages and shelves containing innumerable bottles, whilst under the window was a large sink and bench, obviously used for dispensing. In the wall opposite were large cupboards, and near the fireplace was a table upon which were the remnants of a hasty meal. Two or three chairs made up the rest of the furniture.

It was growing dusk, so she snapped on the electric light switch by the door. This, she felt should convince anyone that she did not seek concealment, and that her presence in the place was not for some dishonest motive.

The only sound emanated from an old-fashioned, noisy wall clock, and once again Miss Frayle stood nonplussed as to what she had better do next. Then she caught sight of the telephone perched on a roll-top desk in a corner near the fire. If she rang up Doctor Morelle and explained the position, she argued to herself, perhaps he would suggest some other chemist. Or he might even have some idea where Mr. Jordan was likely to be found. At any rate, those saturnine features would not be visible at the other end of the wire. She was assailed by doubts once more. Suppose Mr. Jordan came in and found her using his telephone? Well, she would have to explain that's all, she told herself. It would be embarrassing, but a vision of the Doctor awaiting her return with increasing impatience spurred her to action. She went over to the instrument and dialled.

In a moment there came Doctor Morelle's familiar tones:

'Yes?'

'Oh Doctor Morelle, it's me,' she stammered. 'I mean it's I — Miss Frayle — ' She hastily corrected her grammatical error and prayed he hadn't noticed it. All he said was:

'I am not incapable of recognising that the sounds impinging on my ears emanate from your vocal chords,' his voice crackled over the wire. 'From where are you telephoning?'

'Mr. Jordan's. I'm upstairs in his laboratory. He isn't here.'

'Then where is he?'

'I — I'm afraid I don't know.'

'Who admitted you then?'

'I knocked and rang, but no one answered. I tried the side door and as it wasn't locked I went in. I called out, still no reply. Then I thought he might be working upstairs so I came up. But no one's here at all.' She drew a deep breath. 'I've telephoned to know if you would like me to wait till Mr. Jordan comes back or — '

Doctor Morelle heard her break off with a sharp intake of breath, then give a terrified scream.

'Miss Frayle!'

There came another scream, which died into a moan. Followed a clattering thud, as if the telephone receiver had fallen.

'Miss Frayle — what is it! Answer me — what happened?' He waited a moment or two, then murmured to himself. 'Confounded nuisance she is! Here am I waiting to proceed with my experiment . . . Frightened by a mouse no doubt . . . ' He flashed the receiver bar impatiently . . . 'Hello . . . ? Miss Frayle . . . ?' After one more attempt, he replaced the instrument.

'Ah, well,' he snapped to himself, 'I suppose I had better go round and revive her.'

It was now dark outside, and he might have had some little difficulty in finding the chemist's side door, but for the fact that he had his narrow examination torch with him. The door was as Miss Frayle had found it, half-open. He walked in quickly, called: 'Is anyone there?' Then made his way swiftly upstairs. By his torch he could see the door slightly open at the top of the stairs. He went in, found the switch and flooded the room with light, to reveal Miss Frayle lying crumpled by the desk.

In her fall, she had somehow contrived to wrench the telephone receiver from its cord, and the useless instrument lay on the floor. He picked it up and placed it on the desk, then turned his attention to Miss Frayle. She was still unconscious. Her face was ashen. He picked her up and laid her flat on an old couch that ran along one side of the room. Then he opened the window. Within a few moments she began to show signs of recovery. She moaned once or twice, then opened her eyes and blinked at him. She pushed her spectacles, which had fallen awry back into position. Fortunately they had not been broken.

'Oh, Doctor, I must have fainted . . . I'm so sorry . . . '

'Why apologise?' he retorted with heavy sarcasm. 'You are little more than semi-conscious at any time!' She passed her hand over her forehead in bewilderment, then struggled into a sitting position. He steadied her. He continued:

'However, perhaps you can recall what caused you *completely* to lose consciousness?'

She looked up at him in utter bewilderment for a moment. Then suddenly her eyes dilated with horror behind her spectacles and she swung her feet to the floor. She clutched at his arm:

'Where — where is it?'

He regarded her narrowly.

'Where is what?'

'The body! It fell out of that cupboard over there.' She shuddered, and for a second looked as if she might be about to faint again. 'It was horrible! Horrible!'

'Come, come!' said Doctor Morelle sharply. 'Pull yourself together! As you can see, there is no body anywhere.'

Miss Frayle blinked short-sightedly.

'But I saw it! While I was 'phoning you, the cupboard door over there started to open — it's open now — '

'Cupboards have opened before now as a result of traffic vibration from the street.'

'That's what made me scream,' she went on, not listening to his suggested explanation. The picture of what she had seen was too vivid in her mind. 'When the door had swung open, the man fell out — and I fainted.'

'Can you recall what he looked like?'

'His face was ghastly . . . there was blood on the side of his head . . . his hair was grey . . . he had a moustache . . . oh, it was terrible!' She shuddered once more. 'Do you think it might have been Mr. Jordan?' she asked.

'He could answer to that very incomplete description,' he agreed, but there was doubt in his voice. He said smoothly:

'There is, however, an aspect of this case which interests me particularly, Miss Frayle. Briefly it is how you managed to distinguish this man's appearance in the dark.'

Miss Frayle sat straight upright with a jerk.

'In the dark?'

Doctor Morelle nodded, a sardonic expression on his face. 'Yes, my *dear* Miss Frayle. When I arrived here this room was in complete darkness. While it may have been only dusk when you arrived here, still it would not have been light enough for you to observe — '

'But I put the light on when I came in,' she said. And added quickly: 'Otherwise, how would I have seen to telephone?'

He regarded her closely. There was no doubt about the certainty with which she spoke. She went on.

'Somebody must have come into the room while I was unconscious — and moved the body. And they switched out the light when they went out.'

'H'm, that would have been possible, I suppose.' He conceded the point reluctantly. He was annoyed that her explanation would cause him to abandon his theory that Miss Frayle had been suffering from some stupid hallucination. 'I wish you would adjust your spectacles, instead of blinking at me in that astigmatic fashion,' he snapped suddenly.

They had slipped again in Miss Frayle's excited vehemence. She put them into position once more. Meanwhile the Doctor was carefully examining the cupboard she had indicated. He discovered a small, dark, wet stain that might have been blood.

He surveyed the rest of the room. Standing on a small cupboard near the sink he found a bowl containing two or three goldfish. 'Somewhat incongruous,' he mused. 'Mr. Jordan's laboratory would appear to be adequately equipped.' His gaze rested upon a collection of test tubes and various chemical apparatus. To his experienced eye they told him the chemist had obviously been engaged in research work of some nature.

He moved over to the table and gave a cursory glance at the remains of Mr. Jordan's tea, which had been laid on a check cloth covering only half the table's surface. He was about to pass on when he noticed a cigarette-end almost concealed by a folded evening newspaper. It had apparently burnt itself out on the edge of the table.

'Do you recall noticing this before?' he asked Miss Frayle, pointing to the cigarette end. She shook her head.

'Then perhaps you will assist me to look for an ashtray.'

Puzzled by his request, Miss Frayle nevertheless obeyed. They searched every likely place during the next few minutes. At length, having failed to find any ashtray, he murmured:

'It would appear indicative that Mr. Jordan is — or was — a non-smoker. That might, in turn, suggest he recently entertained a visitor who did smoke.'

'Yes — yes, that would be it,' agreed Miss Frayle enthusiastically. 'Perhaps we could trace the man that way — if we could find out the make of cigarette — ' she concluded somewhat vaguely.

'I had already ascertained the name of the manufacturers of the brand in question,' replied the Doctor with a frosty smile. 'As, however, I imagine they sell the better part of a million a day of this particular brand this knowledge would not seem to be of much assistance to us!'

Miss Frayle subsided.

Doctor Morelle continued to survey the room in search of some sort of clue. Finally, he went to the window. With some difficulty he managed to open it to its full extent, and stood looking out on the yard of the garage below. It was moonlight. 'I wonder,' he mused, 'if the body could have been removed by way of this window?'

Miss Frayle joined him and too looked out.

'It isn't very high from the ground,' she said helpfully. He nodded and thoughtfully lit a cigarette. 'It is just possible that man cleaning his car down there may have noticed something unusual.'

'I'll call him,' said Miss Frayle promptly, and proceeded to do so. The man looked up and replied in a cockney accent. He wore overalls, but there was a taxi-driver's hat perched on the back of his head.

'Wot's the trouble?' he asked, looking up from his work.

'Er — do you — have you . . . ?' Miss Frayle became incoherent, not knowing what question would be quite the one to ask. Doctor Morelle unceremoniously edged her aside.

'During this evening, have you, by any chance, observed a person or persons descending from this window?' he said.

The man eyed him quizzically, then pushed his cap even further back on his head.

'No, guv'nor, I ain't seen no person or persons. I ain't seen nobody. But then I been inside the garridge this last 'alf-hour, cleaning up the old taxi. I reckons to give 'er a sluice twice a week, and it's usually about this time, on account of business bein' a bit slack. So I takes this opportunity to — '

'Quite so,' Doctor Morelle cut short the garrulous explanation.

'I can't say as I've ever seen anybody climb out o' that window,' pursued the taxi-driver. 'But wiv' that spout,' he waved in the direction of where a rain-spout might be, 'it shouldn't be much trouble — especially to one of these cat burglars. Why — is there anything wrong?'

'Nothing wrong,' replied the Doctor and pulled down the window.

'There would not appear to be any egress in that direction,' he murmured.

'Wasn't he smoking a cigarette?' asked Miss Frayle. 'I saw the glow of it I'm sure.'

'That fact alone would not necessarily implicate him in this affair,' replied the Doctor acidly. 'At this moment, there are probably several million people in London, including the murderer, smoking a cigarette. Even I am indulging in the pernicious habit!'

With a saturnine smile he flicked the ash of his Le Sphinx. Then he leaned against the edge of the table and surveyed the room once more. Miss Frayle regarded him anxiously.

'What are you going to do now, Doctor? Don't you think we ought to notify the police?'

'All in good time, my dear Miss Frayle, all in good time! First, I wish to consider the evidence so far manifest. There are several quite amateurish aspects of this case which should not render the mystery particularly difficult to elucidate.'

'Well, I don't quite see that we're getting much further . . . Perhaps if the police could examine some fingerprints or — '

'Such elementary routine, while it may serve to fire your somewhat fevered imagination, would merely hinder the process of deduction at this stage.'

He took out his magnifying glass and examined another blotch on the floor, just outside the cupboard from which Miss Frayle had seen the body fall. For the greater part uncovered, the floor was marked with stains of all sizes and descriptions, but this particular one seemed to be fresh, and also had the appearance of blood.

'No doubt a slight effusion from the wound when the body fell,' he murmured thoughtfully. 'If only you could have contrived to retain control of your senses at that moment, Miss Frayle.'

'But I've never seen a body fall from a cupboard like that before, Doctor!' she protested.

'I hope you are now satisfied. But that is of no assistance to me in discovering the identity of — '

He was interrupted by a ring at the side door bell.

Miss Frayle jumped. 'Oh — what's that?' she cried.

His mouth twisted into a smile. 'Merely the result of electrical impetus upon a mechanical device, actuated through pressure applied by a human agency upon another mechanical device!'

Miss Frayle goggled at him through her spectacles as one word magniloquently followed its predecessor.

'You mean it's the door bell?' she managed to murmur at last.

'Precisely. Miss Frayle!'

He stubbed out his cigarette.

'Who is it, I wonder?' she asked.

'That,' he said suavely, 'may be ascertained by proceeding to the door in question and opening it.'

'I'll go.' But he motioned to her to remain where she was.

'I would rather you remained here — and sat down,' he said.

'Thank you, Doctor.' She gave him a grateful look. 'I am still feeling a bit shaky.'

'Do not misunderstand me,' he replied quickly as he made for the door. 'I am merely anxious to avoid the irritation of your again losing that little consciousness with which you are normally endowed!'

Miss Frayle, however, no longer appeared to be paying attention.

'Listen!' she whispered, her eyes widening. 'Whoever it is, they've got tired of waiting.'

There was a sound of footsteps ascending the wooden stairs.

'Alfred — you there?' called a man's voice.

Doctor Morelle, who had paused at the door and stood waiting, made no reply.

Miss Frayle breathed: 'It's a man!'

'Brilliant, Miss Frayle!' the Doctor said without taking his eyes off the door,

In a moment the door opened. A short, thickset man, wearing a bowler hat stood there. He removed it to reveal light, almost sandy hair. His eyebrows seemed to be non-existent, and he boasted a straggly sandy moustache. His blue suit was rather shabby, and inclined to be shiny at the elbows. His rather bleary eyes were somewhat shifty, and as he saw them he appeared to assume an air of confident ease that seemed to require of him not a little effort.

'Hello, what's all this?' he exclaimed heartily, as he came into the room.

'Good evening,' replied the Doctor smoothly, waiting for a further explanation.

'Isn't Alfred — Mr. Jordan here?' demanded the visitor.

'I fear I cannot tell you.' Doctor Morelle surveyed the newcomer with narrowed eyes calculated to make anyone feel uncomfortable.

'He — he's disappeared,' Miss Frayle said.

'Disappeared?' repeated the man. 'How d'you mean: 'disappeared'? I expect he's popped out to see one of his pals, more likely than not. Or a customer, maybe. He's sure to be back soon. You see he was expecting me. I'm his brother-in-law, by the way. Green's my name.'

'I am Doctor Morelle, and this is my assistant, Miss Frayle.'

Green nodded.

'Have you been here long, Doctor?'

'Some considerable time. I — er — wanted a particular acid from him at rather short notice. But he seems to have vanished in somewhat odd circumstances. A cigarette?'

Green shook his head.

'No thanks — don't smoke. Funny old Alfred isn't here. It was rather a particular matter of business I wanted to see him about. I wonder if he got my message wrong? Thought he was to meet me round at my place?'

He raised the hand holding his bowler

and scratched his sandy head.

'This is a blooming nuisance! Taken me half-an-hour to get here, and now he's out. I wish I knew if he'd gone to my place.' He gave Doctor Morelle a genial grin, who coldly ignored it, and went on to suggest:

'I suppose there is no possibility of telephoning your residence in order to ascertain whether or not he is there?'

'Er — yes — could do that — if his 'phone here had been working.'

'Doubtless there is a callbox within easy reach?'

'Just round the comer, there is as a matter of fact.'

'We will go out together,' said Doctor Morelle. 'If you will excuse me a moment . . . '

He went to the window and flung it open. The taxi-man was busily polishing the radiator of his cab.

'You again, guv'nor?' he grinned, looking up.

'Would you bring your taxi round to the front immediately?'

'Okay — couple of shakes! Just give me

time to get me coat on . . . '

The Doctor closed the window.

'But why do we want a taxi, Doctor?' Miss Frayle asked, a puzzled expression on her face.

'For the purpose of transit to the nearest Police Station,' replied Doctor Morelle deliberately.

She glanced quickly at Green who had swung round at the last two words.

'Police Station?' he repeated. 'What's on your mind, Doctor?'

Doctor Morelle showed no sign of perturbation. 'I have an idea the mystery of the missing Mr. Jordan will very soon be elucidated,' he replied evenly. 'Elucidated by me, of course — after which it will be merely a matter of form to hand the culprit over to the appropriate authorities.'

'Anyone would think there's been some sort of crime,' the other expostulated. 'Just because old Alfred pops up the road — '

'If you will come down and make your telephone call, perhaps you may be able to give us some further information regarding Mr. Jordan's movements?'

'Yes — all right — I'm ready,' agreed the other, moving towards the door. 'I hope nothing has happened to him,' he went on. 'But I'm sure you're taking it too seriously.'

'Possibly,' said Doctor Morelle curtly, turning to Miss Frayle.

'Perhaps you will wait here for the taxi-driver and direct him to the telephone box? We shall be awaiting him.'

'Yes — of course, Doctor Morelle.'

The Doctor followed Green down the narrow stair. Miss Frayle came after them. They went out through the side door and Doctor Morelle and the other went off. She waited at the front of the shop until the taxi appeared.

The Doctor and Green reached the callbox, and the man went inside to make his call.

While he was speaking on the telephone, the taxi drove up, Miss Frayle opened the door to find the Doctor waiting quietly smoking a cigarette.

'Have you really discovered the murderer of Mr. Jordan?' she asked him in a whisper with a hurried glance at the man in the callbox.

'Indubitably, my dear Miss Frayle. He is at present quite busily occupied inside this telephone box.' She gasped and he proceeded smoothly: 'We may have a little difficulty in persuading him to visit the Police Station. However — '

Miss Frayle interrupted him. 'Don't worry about that, Doctor Morelle! We shall have no trouble at all!'

He gave her a quick, quizzical look.

'I am afraid I fail to comprehend you, Miss Frayle. Perhaps you will kindly — ?'

Again she interrupted him. This time a triumphant smile lit up her face.

'There isn't much to explain, Doctor,' she said. 'Simply that I've brought a policeman with me!'

And she indicated the stalwart figure of a Police constable who was at that moment clambering out of the taxi.

* * *

It was an hour later that Miss Frayle, waiting in the study of the house in

Harley Street, heard the front door open, and Doctor Morelle came in. She rushed into the hall to greet him

'Did he confess?' she gasped excitedly.

'Pray control your exuberance, Miss Frayle,' he replied calmly, dissecting himself of hat and coat with maddening deliberation.

'But the man Green — did he kill his brother-in-law?'

'Of course.' Doctor Morelle led the way into the study with Miss Frayle hurrying after him. He seated himself at the chair at the desk.

'The mystery proved quite simple when reduced to its elementals,' he said, taking a Le Sphinx from the skull that had been ingeniously made into a somewhat macabre-looking cigarette box.

'Under pressure, Green confessed he had paid a visit to his brother-in-law shortly after eight-thirty this evening, quarreled with him over financial matters and struck him down. This occurred just at the moment you arrived at the side door and rang the bell.'

'Of course, you heard nothing — even

if your mind had been alert,' he added sardonically. He went on: 'Realising there was no time to be lost, he pushed Jordan's body into the cupboard and at the same time secreted himself there.'

Miss Frayle shuddered. 'How awful — if I'd known that horrible man was in there . . . '

The Doctor lit his cigarette. 'It must have been a cramped space,' he continued through a cloud of cigarette smoke, 'hence the door burst open, with the result that you fainted. During your period of unconsciousness, Green dragged the body to another room, from where it has now been recovered. My rapid arrival upset his calculations, and he left the premises, planning to return later to dispose of the body. Then he recalled he had left his cigarette. He *did* indulge in the tobacco-smoking habit after all — '

'Yes, I know,' she smiled.

'Indeed?' His eyebrows were raised in inquiry. 'May I ask how you formed that opinion.'

'I noticed nicotine stain on his moustache.'

'Yes, yes, quite obvious, of course!' Doctor Morelle said, in a tone of annoyance. 'That roused my suspicions, too. He was fearful the remains of the cigarette would incriminate him and he returned hoping to regain it. My suspicions were confirmed by his complete lack of surprise when he referred to the telephone being out of order. This inferred he must have been in the room earlier in the evening to have observed this fact.' He paused dramatically: '*In the room between the time you used the telephone and my* arrival! How otherwise could he have known so conclusively it was damaged?'

Miss Frayle nodded vigorously. 'Of course!' she said.

He said with a thin smile: 'And now, my *dear* Miss Frayle . . . I am anxious to resume my experimental work in the laboratory at the point where unfortunately our attention was distracted.'

She looked at him with a slightly dazed expression.

'But — but Doctor,' she stammered, 'the acid?'

He paused with his cigarette halfway to his lips. 'Do you mean to inform me,' he said, his voice sharp and bitter, 'that you have omitted to obtain another phial to replace the one you so carelessly broke?'

She goggled at him. 'Well — I — I — Yes, I didn't — ' She broke off, floundering.

'Really, your careless inattention to your work is most reprehensible — '

'I'm so sorry, Doctor,' she apologised. But even as she spoke she realised it was no good. She could not prevent that flow of pompously precise words of censure that began to fall from his lips. Miss Frayle sighed resignedly and sat down to wait until Doctor Morelle finished the tirade directed against her.

4

Dr. Morelle and the Nursing Home

It was five minutes past nine on a fine sunny morning in London. Crowds of hurrying office workers were swarming across London Bridge. Amongst the crowd a young fair-haired woman was trying, as best she could, to outpace the other pedestrians.

Miss Frayle glanced up in the direction of the clock, and a spasm of anxiety distorted her features. She desperately tried to accelerate still further, and, in doing so, caught the handle of her umbrella in a bowler-hatted man's arm, nearly pulling him off his feet.

'Oh, I'm most dreadfully sorry!' Miss Frayle apologized.

The irate man had instinctively bunched his fists aggressively as he spun round to face his assailant, but on seeing a genuinely contrite young woman he relaxed.

With a snort of derision, he turned and resumed his interrupted journey.

Somewhat chastened, Miss Frayle proceeded in the opposite direction, a little more slowly than hitherto.

She was quite breathless and disheveled when she eventually arrived at her destination in Harley Street. Hurrying along the road she reached the particular house she was seeking, and mounted the steps leading to the doorway.

She paused briefly, staring at the brass plates on the wall by the doorframe. Prominent among them was one bearing the name so familiar to her: DR. MORELLE.

Miss Frayle searched feverishly in her bag for her latchkey. In the process, she dropped the entire contents on the steps, including the key.

Just as she had recovered her property and was about, at last, to insert the key in the keyhole, the door opened from the inside, and Miss Frayle had to step aside, quickly, to avoid being knocked down by a large man who was being shown out by a white-coated doctor's receptionist.

'*Good* morning,' said the receptionist.

'Good morning,' muttered the man as he went down the steps.

The receptionist looked at Miss Frayle amusedly.

'Hello, Miss Frayle! Late again!'

'It's only a minute or two past nine,' Miss Frayle retorted, hurrying past into the hall.

The Receptionist closed the door, and looked at her watch. 'It's a quarter past, actually. That gentleman was our nine o'clock appointment.'

Miss Frayle gave her a triumphant glance. 'We never see patients before 10 a.m. on Monday. That's Dr. Morelle's rule.'

The receptionist smiled faintly. 'Well, I hope for your sake he hasn't got that Monday morning feeling!'

She disappeared down the hall, while Miss Frayle, gulping nervously, went to the door of Dr. Morelle's Consulting Room and knocked.

There was no reply. Miss Frayle knocked again, with a similar negative result. After a moment's pause she pushed the door gently open and peered round its edge. To her infinite relief, she found the room to be empty. She crossed swiftly to the desk and put her bag down on it.

Then, in uncovering her typewriter, she inadvertently knocked against the dictaphone standing beside it. She failed to notice that she had accidentally switched it on, and that there was a roll already in position. Consequently, she nearly jumped out of her skin when suddenly Morelle's voice boomed out.

'Good morning, Miss Frayle! Late again!'

Miss Frayle gasped as the voice continued: 'I suppose I must resign myself to your constitutional inability to be punctual on Monday mornings. What is your excuse this time?'

Miss Frayle automatically defended herself. 'My . . . my train was late . . . it was foggy . . . '

The recorded voice resumed: 'Fog on the line, I suppose . . . and the inevitable alibi on our British Railways.'

'Oh!' Miss Frayle gave an annoyed gasp.

'You perceive, Miss Frayle,' said the mechanical voice, 'how accurately I can forecast your reactions! There is no doubt in my mind that in a moment your poor dim-witted mind — '

With a snort of anger, Miss Frayle switched off the dictaphone. She crossed over to Dr. Morelle's desk and picked up the morning's mail.

She looked through it to see if there was a note for her. Coming back to her desk, she looked angrily at the dictaphone and sat down and started opening the letters.

But eventually her curiosity was too much for her — she had to know if there was a message for her on that record. So she switched it on again.

' . . . will prompt you to switch off in a childish rage. Soon, however, you will switch on again, if only because your innate curiosity will make you want to discover why I am not with you in the room. In actual fact, I am in the Metropolitan Hospital, where I arrived on Friday evening . . . '

'The Metropolitan Hospital . . . ' Miss

Frayle was aghast, and switched off the Dictaphone again. 'The Metropolitan Hospital!'

Hastily grabbing her handbag and gloves from her desk, she made a dash for the door.

Flinging the door open, she collided with two small children on the step, whose mother had just been about to ring the bell . . .

★ ★ ★

The anxious, hurrying figure of a fair-haired young woman entered the Metropolitan Hospital.

Inside the hospital, Doctor Morelle reclined in a bed situated against the wall of a room containing a good deal of experimental apparatus.

The curtains were drawn across the window, and the only illumination came from a bedside lamp on a small table at the side of the bed. The subdued lighting gave the apparatus a somewhat sinister and eerie aspect.

Leaning over Doctor Morelle was a

male hospital research worker. Nearby, a Hospital nurse stood in attendance. The man was examining Doctor Morelle's eyes with an electric pencil-torch apparatus. The nurse began taking notes at his dictation.

'Dilation 73 . . . general vision normal. It *is* normal, Doctor Morelle?'

'Correct, Tamplin,' his patient responded.

'Good,' murmured Tamplin, checking various electrical leads connected to portions of Doctor Morelle's anatomy. 'I think we can switch on again, nurse.'

'One moment,' Doctor Morelle interjected. 'Blood pressure first, surely?'

'You're right,' Tamplin conceded. 'So sorry.' He picked up the blood-pressure gauge, and began to adjust it on Doctor Morelle's arm.

At that moment there was a knock at the door, and the Nurse went to answer it.

'I do hope you appreciate, Doctor Morelle, how really grateful we all are to you,' Tamplin remarked, as he began to pump up the bandage.

'I've always been keenly interested in

Research,' Doctor Morelle answered.

'But for a man of your qualifications to come here as a human guinea-pig . . . '

'Only a qualified man can react satisfactorily to these tests,' Doctor Morelle pronounced.

Tamplin nodded. 'That's perfectly true. Thanks to you, these tests will tell us authoritatively how long it is possible to resist sleep without impairing the faculties.'

Doctor Morelle smiled thinly. 'After 48 hours all I'm conscious of is a tendency to irritability.'

'Very natural,' Tamplin nodded again, as he deflated the bandage. Then, reading the gauge: 'Definitely high.'

'That's as it should be,' Doctor Morelle commented.

'There's a young woman outside, asking for you, Doctor Morelle,' the nurse announced, turning back from the doorway.

'A young woman?' Doctor Morelle raised his eyebrows.

'She says she's your secretary,' the Nurse added.

Tamplin frowned. 'She must wait. Switch on, please, nurse.'

The Nurse dutifully crossed to the apparatus.

The door to the room was gently pushed open and Miss Frayle appeared, anxiously peering into the room.

'I should have guessed,' Doctor Morelle remarked sardonically. 'Only the word 'young' rather misled me.'

Miss Frayle bit her lip in evident distress as her wide eyes absorbed the rather strange tableau. As the Nurse switched on the electrical apparatus, there came disconcerting cracklings and electric sparks.

Doctor Morelle had closed his eyes, and it was this action that prompted Miss Frayle to dash to his bedside.

'Doctor Morelle! What's the matter with you?'

Doctor Morelle remained motionless.

'Now, really, Miss — ' Tamplin protested.

'I told you to wait,' the Nurse admonished.

'He's dying!' Miss Frayle cried. 'I'm sure he's dying!'

'Now come along with me,' the Nurse said firmly, trying to grasp Miss Frayle's arm. But the agitated secretary threw off her hand and once again leaned over Doctor Morelle, an agonized expression on her face.

The Doctor remained motionless with his eyes closed.

'Speak to me!' Miss Frayle implored him. 'Please speak to me!'

'Go away!' he rasped, still with his eyes closed.

'Oh!'

Tamplin intervened, 'I really can't allow Doctor Morelle to be disturbed like this.'

'I've got to know what's the matter with him!' Miss Frayle persisted. 'Whether he's going to recover — '

Doctor Morelle opened his eyes and wearily shook his head. 'Now, Tamplin, it's more than a *tendency* to irritability. But I'll try and control myself. This unbalanced female whom Nurse was generous enough to describe as a young woman is in fact my secretary. I'll see her for five minutes.'

Tamplin and the Nurse rather reluctantly left the room. Frowning fiercely, Doctor Morelle glared at the flustered Miss Frayle. 'Now, Miss Frayle, will you kindly explain — '

'Tell me you're all right first. Tell me why you're here.'

Doctor Morelle sighed heavily. 'You must have started to play the dictaphone record, otherwise you wouldn't be here. But I assume you didn't bother to hear it right through.'

'Of course I did. And when you mentioned this hospital — '

'You rushed along without waiting till the end,' Doctor Morelle said heavily. 'If you had done so, you'd have heard, that I had arranged to come in here to assist in certain experiments, and that I should be away for about a week.'

Miss Frayle looked horrified.

'You're not letting them experiment on you?'

'That's my business!' the Doctor snapped tersely. 'I told you that in no circumstances was I to be disturbed.'

'I'm not disturbing you. It's very lucky

I have come before these horrible risky experiments permanently injure your health.'

'I'm perfectly capable of looking after my health.'

Miss Frayle was now thoroughly worked up.

'Oh, no, you're not. Look at you! Why, you look as if you hadn't had a wink of sleep since last Friday!'

With an expression of extreme irritability, Doctor Morelle sat up in bed and pointed to the door with a shaking finger.

'Get out!' he yelled.

'But, Doctor — '

'Get out before I throw you out.'

'But I can't leave you like this,' Miss Frayle protested tearfully. 'What can I do to help you?'

Doctor Morelle summoned a supreme effort at self-control.

'Miss Frayle, the only way you can help me is to go straight back to Harley Street, answer my letters, see to my appointments for next week and generally behave like a normal secretary instead of . . . ' Here his voice rose in an ever-growing crescendo as his control slipped, ' . . . fluttering about here like an orphaned budgerigar!'

★　★　★

Miss Frayle was lying back langorously in Doctor Morelle's chair, reading the newspaper, her feet resting on the desk.

Suddenly she gave an exclamation of horror as she stared at the newspaper. She was gazing at a police photograph of a man, front face and two profiles. Underneath it was a caption, which Miss Frayle read aloud to herself:

' . . . 'Arthur Mason. Have you seen this man? The police are anxious to interview him in connection with the bank robbery in Paddington in which a cashier and two women employees were fatally shot'. How terrible!'

The next instant the telephone rang,

Pushing aside a heap of unopened letters lying on the desk, Miss Frayle put the paper down and picked up the receiver.

'Hello . . . Yes, this is Doctor Morelle's

secretary . . . Hello, Miss Hadden . . . what can we do for you . . . No, I'm afraid the doctor's away this week . . . your letter? I don't remember any letter . . . Hold on a minute . . . '

She glanced down at the pile of unopened correspondence, and tucking the receiver under her chin and bending her head sideways to hold it in position, she hastily slit open the letters until she found Miss Hadden's.

' . . . Are you there, Miss Hadden? I've found your letter. The doctor must have tucked it away without telling me, the naughty man . . . Of course I'll fix an appointment for you, Miss Hadden . . . As soon as the doctor returns. Actually, he's far from well . . . Yes, works much too hard . . . You're quite right, Miss Hadden. That's just what he needs. A few day absolute rest in a nice Convalescent Home . . . Yes, Miss Hadden . . . No, Miss Hadden . . . '

Miss Frayle looked round as she heard the door opening, and the receptionist from across the hall peeped in. Becoming bored with her caller, Miss Frayle signalled her to come in.

'Very well, Miss Hadden, goodbye
. . . thank you so much . . . Goodbye,
Miss Hadden.'

With a sigh of relief she hung up and
turned to the receptionist.

'I thought I'd never get rid of her! What
can I do for you, dear?'

'Have you got any nail varnish?' the
receptionist asked.

'Nail varnish?' Miss Frayle was surprised.

'My boyfriend's picking me up here at
six, and one of my nails has peeled.'

'I always keep mine here,' said Miss
Frayle, rising and crossing to a cupboard.
She opened the door.

Following her, the receptionist was
disconcerted to find the cupboard full of
bottles and phials, and the top shelf
carrying a label 'Poison'.

Miss Frayle pulled out a small bottle
from the poison shelf, and handed it to
the receptionist. The latter regarded it
doubtfully.

'You're quite sure — '

'You needn't worry,' Miss Frayle reas-
sured her. 'I keep it there so the doctor

won't notice it. What about the colour?'

'Wonderful! It's an exact match.'

Miss Frayle beamed, 'Good. Then you can fix up straightaway.'

The two women moved back to the desk. The receptionist sat on the end, and proceeded to paint her nail, whilst Miss Frayle began tidying up the letters.

The receptionist asked: 'What's the news of your old man?'

Miss Frayle bristled slightly. 'That's no way to speak of Doctor Morelle. Besides, he's not old.'

The receptionist shrugged slender shoulders. 'Anything over 40 creaks. When'll he be back?'

'It's hard to say exactly.' Miss Frayle wrinkled her brow. 'What he needs is a proper convalescence.'

'He ought to try Clymping Court,' the receptionist remarked.

'Clymping Court?'

'Yes. Not far from Maidenhead. It's been strongly recommended to us.'

Miss Frayle was interested. 'Really? Who runs it?'

'Man from Vienna. Count Otto somebody.

He's brilliant, they say.' The receptionist finished off her nail, blew on it, then stood up. 'Thanks ever so. Shall I put it back?'

Miss Frayle shook her head. 'Don't bother dear.'

The receptionist put the bottle down on the desk, then paused as the photograph in the newspaper caught her eye. 'He looks like a killer, doesn't he?'

Miss Frayle gave a start. 'Who does?'

The receptionist pointed to the picture. 'I always say, it's written in their faces. That's why I'm so choosy with my boyfriends.'

As the receptionist turned towards the door, Miss Frayle called after her:

'What was the name of that Convalescent Home again?'

'Clymping Court.'

After the girl had left, Miss Frayle remained deep in thought for a few moments. At length she rose, and went to the bookshelf. Here she pulled out a copy of the *Railway A.B.C.*

★　★　★

From where Miss Frayle stood in the lane, Clymping Court presented an imposing and impressive aspect. Her gaze moved to an ornate notice board hanging on a wrought-iron framework:

CLYMPING COURT CONVALESCENT HOME: OCCUPATIONAL THERAPY.

Miss Frayle slowly approached the front door. Judging by her rather hesitant progress, it was apparent that she was somewhat overawed by the size and magnificence of the house.

When she was only a few yards from the door, an ambulance swept into the drive and drew up outside the front door. Having drawn aside to let it pass, Miss Frayle stood unobserved by the bushes at the edge of the drive.

It was evident that the ambulance had been expected, because as the driver and attendant got out the front door opened and a benevolent-looking white-haired man appeared, accompanied by the uniformed doorkeeper. Miss Fayle surmised that the white-haired man must be Count Otto.

The ambulance driver and attendant

came round to the back of the vehicle and opened the doors. Miss Frayle watched as they lifted out a stretcher on which a figure was lying, covered by a blanket. The blanket covered the figure's face, causing Miss Frayle to give an involuntary little shiver. Could it be a corpse?

Cautiously she moved forward, so that the ambulance was between her and the front door, placing her out of sight to the white-haired man.

The driver and the attendant started to carry the stretcher round the ambulance, so that their path lay between the vehicle and Miss Frayle.

As Doctor Morelle's secretary stared at the stretcher, she was thoroughly disconcerted as the 'corpse's' hand lifted and pulled the blanket off its face, revealing a man's features.

Miss Frayle felt the cold touch of fear as she recognized the man. It was the same man she had seen featured in the newspaper — Arthur Mason, the bank robber and triple murderer!

The stretcher-bearers carried Mason up to the white-haired man, who hastily pulled the blanket back over Mason's face and accompanied the stretcher into the house.

'Straight through,' he directed. 'Number 10!'

Still concealed from the front door by the ambulance, Miss Frayle beat a hasty retreat, not pausing until she was under cover.

She peered round the bushes, which hid her from the house. In addition to her handbag, she had been carrying a couple of magazines and the daily paper. With shaking hands she dropped the bag and magazines, and eventually managed to get the paper open, in spite of a breeze trying to blow it inside out. She gazed on the photograph of Arthur Mason.

'It's *him* all right!' she breathed.

★ ★ ★

In a hospital bed, Doctor Morelle was lying back on his pillows, his eyes closed and an expression of infinite weariness on his face.

In front of him on the bed lay the

newspaper open at the page containing Mason's picture. By the side of the bed sat an excited Miss Frayle, eagerly pouring out her story.

' . . . I'm *certain* it was Mason! His nose was exactly like that photograph!'

She leaned across the bed to point to the picture and clumsily hit one of the electric wires connected to Doctor Morelle.

'Oh! I'm so sorry!' she exclaimed, and tried to reconnect the wire.

Doctor Morelle opened his eyes and stared at his secretary in speechless disgust.

'There!' she said triumphantly, having managed to connect the disturbed wire with another one.

'As I was saying,' Miss Frayle resumed, 'I've no doubt in my mind. But what I don't understand — '

Suddenly the two electric wires started sizzling and crackling, sparks flying in all directions.

'Oh — good gracious . . .'

'Quick!' Doctor Morelle snapped. 'Switch it off.'

Miss Frayle rushed for the light switch by the door.

'Not there. By the distributor.'

Miss Frayle rushed back across the room, found the switch and turned it off. The sizzling and the crackling and the sparks subsided.

Doctor Morelle gazed at her malevolently.

'Having ruined an experiment which had been building up to its climax over the last 48 hours, and having done your best to electrocute me, I should be obliged, Miss Frayle, if you'll kindly leave me and get out!'

Miss Frayle hesitated. 'I'm so sorry, Doctor. But I must have your advice.'

She moved towards the bed.

'I've given it to you — get out!'

'But surely I ought to do something about it,' Miss Frayle persisted. 'I'm *sure* it was the murderer. What's he doing in a Convalescent Home? Why were they expecting him? They must have been because Room 10 was ready for him. And . . . and what's Occupational Therapy anyway?'

'Occupational Therapy,' Dr. Morelle explained tiredly, 'consists of specially devised exercises to restore normality after an operation, an accident or an illness. It can also be applied to mental processes for such patients who, unlike you, Miss Frayle, *have* a mind.'

'You mean,' Miss Frayle said eagerly, 'that I have — '

Her face fell as she suddenly got his real meaning. 'Oh! I only wanted to know. Because I really am quite sure it's the man.'

Doctor Morelle remained singularly unimpressed.

'Since you are so notoriously incapable of distinguishing between fact and fiction, neither I nor anyone else can be expected to pay any attention to this nonsensical story.'

'It's not nonsense! Don't you see — ' As Miss Frayle gesticulated violently she snapped another of the wires. The snapped wire sprang back and knocked her hat down over her eyes.

'Oh . . . what . . . how dare you . . . ' Miss Frayle pushed her hat back and stared at the grimly smiling Doctor Morelle.

'A good illustration of reflex action — and thoroughly deserved.'

'Then you don't think I ought to go to the Police?'

'Judging by what happens to my affairs when you start interfering, Miss Frayle, I should say it was vital in the interests of British Justice that you should keep out of the way — and stay out.'

'But — '

'Go back to the Consulting Room, sit down at the dictaphone and make a record and then play it back over and over again.'

Miss Frayle was puzzled. 'Make a record? What shall I say?'

'I was born a fool, I've remained a fool, I shall die a fool. Help me, oh Lord, to recognise my foolishness.'

'O-oh!' Miss Frayle was mortally offended. Rapidly collecting the paper, her handbag, the two magazines, and her umbrella, she rose and tried to sweep off in a dignified exit.

Unfortunately the crook of her umbrella

caught in the bedside lamp and brought it crashing down, upsetting everything on the table and nearly causing her to fall.

'Oh dear . . . Oh, I'm sorry . . . '

She was trying to pick things up when the door opened and the Nurse hurried in.

'What on earth — '

'It's quite all right, Nurse,' Doctor Morelle said dryly. 'It's only my secretary trying to make me comfortable.'

Once more overcome with wounded anger, Miss Frayle finally left the room.

The Nurse bent to pick up some of the fallen articles. 'There's a glass broken. I'll get a dustpan.'

As she went to the door, Doctor Morelle called to her:

'Oh, Nurse, bring me any of last week's *Times* that you can find.'

The Nurse turned. 'Certainly. Anything particular you want to look up?'

'I want to glance through the Arthur Mason case — you know, the Paddington Bank Robbery.'

* * *

Back at Doctor Morelle's consulting room, Miss Frayle was making a recording on the Dictaphone. She was dressed for the outdoors, and a suitcase stood on the floor beside her.

' . . . So if things go wrong and I don't return, you will know what has happened to me. Goodbye and God bless you.'

Finishing her recording, she switched on the playback:

'For Doctor Morelle from Miss Frayle. I have decided that it's essential to check the identity of the man in the Convalescent Home. So, as you forbade me to go to the police, I'm going to investigate personally. I've booked a room in the name of Carnegie, and am pretending that I am a concert pianist recovering from a rheumatic affliction in my left hand, which will necessitate a course of Occupational Therapy . . . I hope I shall only be away a week, although if I am right in what I saw and things go wrong . . .'

Miss Frayle nodded to herself and switched the machine off. Then, picking up her suitcase, she left the house.

Outside, she handed the case to the

driver of a hired car that was waiting for her. She got into the vehicle and was driven away.

* * *

Later that day the car containing Miss Frayle reached Clymping Court, just outside Maidenhead. It drove along the approach road and turned in at the gates.

The car driver pulled up and stopped outside the door. Miss Frayle alighted from the vehicle.

As she was paying the driver the door to the house was opened and the door attendant appeared. He took Miss Frayle's suitcase and ushered her inside.

Miss Frayle stared about her with excited interest as she followed the doorkeeper across the hall. There were a few patients sitting about, or strolling up and down the stairs, a nurse or two amongst them. Everything seemed very normal, comfortable and pleasant.

The doorkeeper stopped at a highly polished study door and knocked respectfully.

Inside the study, the white-haired man

Miss Frayle had seen earlier rose from the chair behind his desk and went to open the door.

Bidding Miss Frayle to enter, he exuded charm and sympathy as he spoke to her in a soft persuasive voice with a slight trace of a continental accent.

'Miss Carnegie, is it not?'

'That's right. You are — ?'

'I am Count Otto. That is all you need to call me. I am so glad we should have you here. What a pleasure!'

'It's mutual I'm sure,' Miss Frayle replied nervously.

'And so — you are a musician? How I love music! Now what composer is your favourite — Dvorak?'

Miss Frayle hesitated, completely lost.

'Or do you love them all, eh?'

'That's — that's right.'

'Soon now we shall cure that poor hand of yours. And then you shall give us a recital of your music.'

Miss Frayle gulped. This was an eventuality for which she had not catered.

'I'm afraid . . . I'm so out of practice . . . '

'But you shall have every opportunity

for practice. That shall be part of your Occupational Therapy. Now I shall introduce you to the doctor who will be in charge of your case, and also your special nurse . . . ' He broke off to ring a bell on the desk.

'But I don't need a nurse,' Miss Frayle demurred.

'Every patient here has a special nurse, Miss Carnegie. To make sure they are comfortable, and also to see that they conform to the rules.'

'Rules?'

Otto laughed genially. 'There is only one rule which is really important, but that one I have to insist upon most strictly. In no circumstances is one patient allowed in another patient's room.'

Whilst Miss Frrayle was pondering this, the door opened and a doctor and nurse entered. They paused for a moment, looking across at Count Otto and Miss Frayle.

The doctor was a man of about 35, good-looking in a dark and slightly sinister fashion.

The nurse with him was a woman in

the middle 20's, neatly dressed, and with an air of efficiency about her. She was attractive, though in a rather hard way.

Count Otto looked up and Miss Frayle turned in their direction.

'Oh, Cortez. Come and meet your new patient. Miss Carnegie, this is Professor Cortez, who is a specialist in rheumatic troubles.'

Miss Frayle smiled bravely. 'How d'you do?'

Although foreign in appearance, there was no trace of accent when Cortez spoke.

'I'm glad to meet you, I believe your trouble has been in your left hand?'

'That's right.'

'I have told Miss Carnegie that soon now we will have her playing the piano,' Count Otto remarked. 'Oh, and this is Nurse Andrews.'

'How d'you do?' Nurse Andrews gave a hard smile.

Count Otto said, 'We will put Miss Carnegie in number 22, Nurse Andrews.'

'Very good, Count.'

Miss Frayle spoke daringly: 'Oh! I'm disappointed.'

'Please?' Count Otto raised an eyebrow.

'I would have liked number 10,' Miss Frayle explained.

The others in the room were suddenly motionless and silent. Their expressions were completely deadpan.

Count Otto broke the silence. 'Why would you prefer No. 10, Miss Carnegie?' he asked, evenly.

By now Miss Frayle was regretting her temerity and was thoroughly alarmed by the vaguely sinister atmosphere that had came over the room.

'Oh, I wasn't really being serious. Ten's my lucky number, that's all.'

'I see,' Count Otto said. 'And now perhaps you would like to see round generally, and then be shown your room?'

'Thank you so much.' There was genuine thankfulness in Miss Frayle's voice at the easing of tension in the room.

'Nurse Andrews will show you round, Miss Carnegie. I have some business with the principal.' He opened the door and Miss Frayle went out, followed by the nurse.

Cortez closed the door, and hurried

across to Count Otto. Both men now appeared to have dropped their professional manners and charm.

'What did she mean — about No. 10?' Cortez said briefly.

'Nothing. Don't fuss.'

'Why did you have to put her on to me and Andrews?' Cortez pursued angrily.

'I could not arrange it otherwise.'

'But we're full up with Specials. And now we've got another urgent job in No. 10 — '

'We're short-handed,' Count Otto retorted. 'You know that. You and Andrews must help. There must be ordinary cases, as well as Specials. It is necessary both financially — and for security.'

The telephone rang and Count Otto picked up the receiver.

'Yes . . . Who? Oh, good afternoon, Sir Henry . . . certainly . . . let me just look . . . ' He quickly checked with a notebook, which was lying on the desk.

' . . . Yes, I could squeeze him in . . . Oh, this afternoon? But . . . Oh, if you say that, Sir Henry, of course . . . Yes, I see . . . What is his name? Carruthers. Yes

. . . goodbye and thank you, Sir Henry.'

He rang off and looked up at Cortez.

'There you are! That was Sir Henry Venables. The best-known heart specialist in Europe! He's sending us a patient — one of his own patients! That shows we're above suspicion!'

Elsewhere in the home, Miss Frayle and Nurse Andrews had entered the main Patients' Lounge. Miss Frayle was noting uneasily that in addition to sofas and armchairs, it contained a grand piano.

Various patients were sitting about, reading and chatting. A few women were knitting. Miss Frayle's gaze swung to one armchair, where a man was sitting, his face entirely obscured by a newspaper.

'This is the Patients' Lounge,' Nurse Andrews said. 'This is where we have lectures and concerts.'

'How nice,' Miss Frayle murmured, her eyes swinging back to the man reading the newspaper, and she moved forward. The nurse followed her.

'You're longing to get at that piano, I expect.'

'Oh, yes! Rather!'

'I'm sure Professor Cortez will soon get your hand better.'

'I hope so.'

'Then we'll be able to enjoy your playing, Miss Carnegie.'

During this exchange, Miss Frayle had been manoeuvring so that she could see round the paper to get a glimpse of the man's face. But just as she was about to succeed, he shifted his position, the paper still between them.

In desperation, Miss Frayle deliberately dropped her handbag into the man's lap.

'Oh, I'm so sorry . . . '

The paper was abruptly lowered, and to Miss Frayle's consternation the man was revealed as a chubby-faced clergyman. By no stretch of the imagination could he be mistaken for Arthur Mason. The clergyman smiled.

'That's quite all right.' He handed back the handbag.

'Thank you,' Miss Frayle said weakly.

Nurse Andrews indicated another part of the room. 'That door leads to the Occupational Therapy room. Would you like to see it?'

'Oh, yes, please.'

They went through the door, emerging into a large room filled with diverse kinds of apparatus used for Occupational Therapy, including ropes for climbing, wall-bars, and a loom.

There were two Therapists in charge, a girl who undertook the more correct and less energetic exercises, such as weaving, and a man who appeared dressed as a Gym instructor. He was concentrating on the rope and ladder climbers, teaching them to go up using the hands only, and come down both right side up and upside down.

Miss Frayle was anxiously scanning the faces of the male patients to see if she could recognise Mason. This led her into making some odd contortions when they were upside down or on the ropes and ladders.

'I expect you'll be put on weaving to start with,' Nurse Andres said.

'Will I really?'

'Oh, Miss Molton!' the nurse called.

The girl Therapist came up and Nurse Andrews turned to introduce her to Miss

Frayle, only to find she had wandered off and was trying to visualise the face of a man who was descending a rope upside down.

The two women came up to her. 'This is Miss Molton, Miss Carnegie,' the nurse introduced.

'How do you do?' Miss Molton said.

Miss Frayle smiled and nodded to her.

'Miss Carnegie is a pianist,' Nurse Andrews told the Therapist.

'How marvellous. I love music.'

'Yes. It is nice, isn't it?'

'Miss Carnegie has had trouble with her wrist,' the nurse continued.

'Which wrist?' Miss Molton asked.

'The left — isn't it?' The nurse turned to where Miss Frayle was, but again she had vanished.

Miss Frayle was by the wall, trying to get a look at a man who was climbing the wall-ladders. She was about to start climbing herself as Nurse Andrews and Miss Molton came up to her again.

'May I have a look at your hand?' the Therapist asked.

'Oh, certainly.'

She held out her right hand.

Miss Molton frowned. 'Then it's the right — not the left?'

'Miss Frayle hastily substituted her left hand. I'm sorry — I didn't realise you meant the bad one.'

Miss Molton examined her hand and gently flexed her fingers to and fro. 'Does that hurt?'

Miss Frayle said 'No,' automatically.

'Does *that* hurt?' Miss Molton increased the pressure.

'No.' Suddenly Miss Frayle realized what she was saying. 'Ouch! That's what catches me.'

'That's what I thought. Not only stops you playing the piano, but hampers you picking anything up.'

'That's right,' Miss Frayle assented. 'I can't really lift anything with this hand.'

'Don't you worry. We'll soon have you absolutely splendid!'

Nurse Andrews said: 'Now perhaps you'd like to see your room?'

'Thank you.'

As they progressed along the outside corridor, Miss Frayle's gaze excitedly noted the numbers on the doors they passed. A little shiver passed through her as they passed doors marked 6 to 8, and they approached the next door, which she anticipated should be No. 10. She stopped as she saw that the number on the door was 12, struggling to keep an expression of first incredulity and then disappointment from her face.

'Miss Carnegie!' Nurse Andrews said sharply.

Miss Frayle didn't recognize her adopted name. She turned to see to whom Nurse Andrews was speaking.

'What's the matter?'

'Er — my silly mistake. I'm 22, aren't I? I thought I was 12.'

Nurse Andrews looked hard at her for a moment, then: 'This way.' She moved off down the corridor, Miss Frayle following her.

At length they reached room 22. The nurse entered, followed by Miss Frayle. Her suitcase was on a luggage stand at the foot of the bed.

'This is your room,' Nurse Andrews said briefly.

'It's very nice,' Miss Frayle said, looking around.

'Shall I help you unpack?'

'Oh no, thank you. I can manage.'

'But what about your bad hand?'

Miss Frayle smiled and held out her right hand. 'I'm used to using one hand.'

'Then I'll leave you. I've other patients as well, you know.'

'Please don't bother about me.'

'You're very kind.' The nurse smiled and went out of the door, closing it behind her.

Miss Frayle again looked round the room. Than she opened the suitcase and began to unpack, using her right hand only. But she soon found that to be very slow and inconvenient. With an exclamation of annoyance, she resumed normal proceedings and used both hands. She picked up a fistful of things in her left hand and carried them across to the dressing table.

In the door, unknown to Miss Frayle, there reposed one of the small observation openings, about 6 inches square, not uncommon in some hospitals and most prisons. Slowly the flap was pulled aside and Nurse Andrews peeped inside. As she watched Miss Frayle, an ugly frown came over her face.

★ ★ ★

Various patients were sitting about the garden in deck chairs. Amongst them Miss Frayle was wandering, trying to appear nonchalant, but actually manoeuvering so that she could get a look at the faces of all the men.

At length she arrived at the last deck chair. Her face registered resigned disappointment and then she suddenly stiffened and stared ahead.

Directly in her line of vision, underneath a shady weeping willow, was another deck chair, its back towards her. In it was a figure, which from the legs visible beneath the chair, was that of a man.

The light of battle in her eye, Miss Frayle started to creep forward. She skirted round the tree and then quietly crept up to the overhanging branches. She carefully pulled aside the branches with her hands, and peered cautiously through the branches, then gasped with sheer disappointment.

The man in the chair had his face entirely covered with bandages, with only two holes for his eyes.

Miss Frayle turned away from the tree and made her way back towards the house.

As Miss Frayle appeared round the corner of the house, a large closed car entered the drive and stopped opposite the front door. The door attendant joined the driver in helping a man out of the car.

He was wearing a coat and a hat pulled forward on his forehead and a muffler round his neck, which effectively concealed his face.

The driver and door attendant supported the man as he walked slowly into the house. Impulsively, Miss Frayle followed them.

In the hall, Count Otto, attended by Nurse Andrews, came forward to greet them.

Miss Frayle hovered in the background. She wanted to get to the stairs but they blocked her way, and she hesitated to push through.

'Ah, Mr. Carruthers,' Count Otto said expansively, and the man nodded and murmured something inarticulate. 'I hope the journey has not tired you too much,'

The man shook his head. He half turned, and on seeing Miss Frayle, quickly turned his back on her.

'I think . . . straight to your room . . . yes?' Count Otto advised. 'Here is Nurse Andrews. She will help you. It's number 4 — on the ground floor.'

The nurse came and took the man's arm, while Count Otto took the other. They moved away from Miss Frayle as she went on up the stairs, and the driver and attendant moved back towards the front door.

Miss Frayle was hurrying along the corridor on the first floor. She proceeded once more to check the numbers on the doors, and to satisfy herself that No. 10 does really seem to be non-existent.

Then round the corner came Cortez.

'There you are, Miss Carnegie,' he exclaimed. 'I've been looking for you everywhere.'

'I'm so sorry, Professor. I've been in the garden.'

Cortez said, 'I want to make a preliminary examination.'

They moved off down the corridor.

★ ★ ★

Later that night, Miss Frayle lay in the bed in her room. It was only lit by moonlight, which filtered in through a chink in the curtains. A distant clock was striking 12. Miss Frayle stirred, switched on the bedside light and verified the time by her travelling clock. She jumped out of bed, put on her dressing gown and slippers. Then she went to the door, gently opened it a few inches, and listened. All was quiet. She slipped out into the corridor.

There was only one dim light at the end. Checking once more that there was no number 10 there, she proceeded to tiptoe downstairs.

She entered the Therapy Room. It was lit only by the moonlight coming through the uncurtained windows. She listened.

At first all was silent. Then there came a mysterious tapping sound. Miss Frayle looked round, terrified. A branch, stirred by the wind, was tapping against the window.

Realising what it was, Miss Frayle breathed a sigh of relief. She started to move across the room to a door, which she could dimly see in the opposite wall.

Suddenly, it seemed to Miss Frayle that a rope had been thrown round her. As she struggled, a second circle of rope curled round her.

She was just about to scream the roof off, as she struggled to free herself, when she realised that she had simply ran into one of the climbing ropes hanging from the ceiling. Disentangling herself, she successfully negotiated the rest of the room and reached the door.

Miss Frayle opened the door and was just about to go through when she heard a strange clicking noise. She peered through, then pulled the door back so that there was only a narrow opening of a few inches through which she could keep observation.

Miss Frayle gasped silently at what she saw in the corridor beyond — two figures standing locked in a passionate embrace.

Professor Cortez and Nurse Andrews!

After a minute or so, Nurse Andrews disengaged herself from her lover's embrace. 'Mark, darling, let's get away from here.'

'All in good time, my sweet.'

'This racket's getting too risky.'

'Maybe,' Cortez conceded. 'But we've got to have the dough. It costs money to get to South America.'

'But, darling, if anything should happen — '

'It won't be long now. We're full up in No. 10. I'm going to sting old Otto good and proper.'

'It's a tricky job.'

'I can do it. There's nothing to worry about.'

Nurse Andrews remained agitated. 'Oh, yes, there is. This Carnegie woman, for instance. I believe she's a phoney.'

'I couldn't find anything wrong with her hand,' Cortez conceded.

'She was using it when she unpacked

without any difficulty.'

'You'd better keep your eye on her, then. Though she strikes me as being too much of a fool to be dangerous.'

Miss Frayle tightened her lips with indignation, but remained silently eavesdropping.

'We'll tell her what she needs is practice, and then see if she *can* play the piano,' Nurse Andrews decided.

Cortez looked at his watch. 'It's late. I must go to No. 10.'

'I'll come with you.'

As they moved down the corridor towards her, Miss Frayle, excited at what she had overheard, was forced to pull the door gently shut in case they saw her. She therefore did not see what happened next.

Cortez and the nurse stopped by a blank wall. He bent down and touched something in the wainscot.

A panel in the wall slid aside, revealing the beginning of a narrow flight of stairs, which twisted downwards. The pair entered, and the panel closed behind them.

Very gently Miss Frayle opened the

door and peeped out. She was flabbergasted to find the corridor was empty. She came out of the doorway and hurried along the corridor in the direction the two people had taken, pausing to listen at various doors. She could not understand where they could have gone.

Suddenly she tensed as she heard the sound of footsteps approaching. She looked about her distractedly, then hurriedly opened the nearest door — No. 4 — and slipped inside and shut it.

The room was in darkness. Miss Frayle leant against the door, holding her breath and listening intently.

Outside, emerging round the corner, appeared a man with a bandaged face. He stopped opposite the secret panel, bent down, and touched the spring in the wainscot. The panel slid open, and he went through. The panel closed behind him.

Going along a short corridor, the bandaged man came to a door marked 10, and knocked. Then he opened the door and went inside.

Meanwhile, inside room No. 4 Miss

Frayle was still listening intently. She gave a gasp of fright when suddenly the light in the room was switched on. Thoroughly alarmed, she swung round, blinking.

Sitting up in bed was none other than Doctor Morelle.

'Oh my God!' Miss Frayle chattered. 'It's a ghost!'

'On the contrary,' the Doctor said dryly, 'I am the one that's being haunted.'

'But you shouldn't be here! You're ill.'

Doctor Morelle smiled sardonically. 'In that case a convalescent home is what I need.'

'But . . . when . . . how . . . I don't understand . . . '

'You'll understand a great deal less if you make so much noise,' the Doctor admonished. 'I've no wish to have *my* throat cut.'

In the subterranean suite behind door No. 10, the man with the bandaged face sat looking about him impatiently. He was in a waiting room, beyond which was a Consulting Room, and a door leading to dressing room and an Operating Theatre, which the man knew from previous visits to be equipped with the most modern surgical apparatus.

His gaze passed over the other four men in the room, the same men whom Miss Frayle had earlier seen in the Therapy Room. They were seated in chairs awaiting their turn in the Theatre.

The door opened, disclosing Nurse Andrews and another man who had finished his interview with the doctor, and who then took a vacant chair.

Nurse Andrews beckoned to the man with the bandaged face.

'You next, please.'

He got up and went into the inner room.

Before the nurse could close the door, two of the other waiting men started protesting.

''Ere, wot's the gime?' the first man growled. 'I came before 'im!'

'The House surgeon wishes to see him first,' Nurse Andrews said shortly.

'It's a bleeting shame!' put in the second man. 'I bleeting well bin waitin' 'alf the bleeting night to see the bleeting doctor!'

'Any more from you and I'll report you to the Superintendent,' Nurse Andrews snapped. She went inside and firmly shut the door.

In Doctor Morelle's bedroom Miss Frayle was concluding her somewhat incoherent chronicle of what she had discovered that evening.

'If only we can find this room number 10, I'm absolutely certain we shall have solved — '

'One minute, please. You say that Nurse Andrews said she was suspicious of you?'

'Yes.'

'I see. Incidentally, do you play the piano?'

'No.'

Doctor Morelle sighed. 'How typical that you should have assumed the role of a pianist!'

'I didn't think — '

'My dear Miss Frayle, you never do. That's why it's imperative that from now on you leave matters to me.'

Miss Frayle was very disappointed. 'You mean, you don't want me to find out anything more?'

'Not a thing.'

'But . . . but what am I going to do?'

'Listen carefully, and I'll tell you.'

In the Consulting Room, Cortez was studying some photographs while Nurse Andrews was replacing the bandages on a man's face.

'Couldn't be better!'

'It's really going to work?' asked the man hopefully.

'Couldn't be shaping more successfully.' Cortez affirmed.

'How much longer before I can see for myself?'

'I'll finish you off tomorrow. Then you ought to be clear in another week or so.'

Nurse Andrews completed the man's bandaging.

'Take him back, Nurse, and get him settled,' Cortez instructed.

'Very good. Will you want me back? I ought to look in on number 4 — the Night Nurse is sick.'

Cortez nodded. 'I can manage.'

As the nurse escorted the bandaged man to the door, Cortez added:

'Send in Perkins, will you?'

The bandaged man and Nurse Andrews

went out, leaving the door open and then Perkins the second man in the Waiting Room, came in.

Cortez looked him over. 'Well, you ought to be ready by now.'

'I bleeting well am,' Perkins exclaimed. 'If I can climb that bleeting rope without usin' me bleeting legs, I reckon I can bleeting well manage a bleeting drainpipe.'

In the ground floor corridor, Nurse Andrews closed the secret panel, watched by the bandaged man. Straightening up, she moved off along the corridor, the man following her. She stopped outside Room No. 4.

'There's a new patient in here. I ought to settle him. You go to your room and get undressed.'

'Very good, sister.'

Inside Doctor Morelle's room, he concluded his instructions to Miss Frayle.

'I tell you you're to lay off all detective work. You aren't capable of doing it.'

Miss Frayle was indignant. 'Of course I am! It was I who saw Mason brought here.'

'You leave Mason to me. From now on

I've taken over. The one absolute essential is that no one should suspect that you and I have ever met before.'

'But, really, Doctor Morelle — '

She broke off in alarm as he suddenly made a fierce gesture to silence her and pointed to the door handle.

It was slowly turning.

Outside, in the corridor, Nurse Andrews, her hand on the door handle, turned it and opened the door a few inches as she gave final instructions to the man with the bandaged face.

'Your shirt last, mind, and take great care you don't shift the bandages.'

'All right, sister.'

Inside the room, Miss Frayle was staring at the gradually opening door.

'Hide!' Doctor Morelle whispered.

Nurse Andrew's voice came from the doorway: 'All right then. You get along.'

As Miss Frayle glanced wildly round the room, Doctor Morelle whispered more urgently, 'Hide!'

'Where?'

'*Under the bed!*'

Miss Frayle made a dive for it and

disappeared from view just as Nurse Andrews entered and came over to the bed.

'I hoped you'd be asleep, Mr. Carruthers.'

'I got off to sleep all right, but unfortunately I was disturbed.'

'What was it? A nightmare?'

'That's right, Nurse. A perfectly horrible nightmare.'

Miss Frayle was lying on her side under the bed, cramped and uncomfortable. She listened to the conversation with growing indignation.

'I have studied the subconscious mind for some years, and I have always been astonished at the revolting nature that nightmares can assume.'

Nurse Andrews was smiling sympathetically at her patient. Evidently she found him an attractive man.

'We'll have to see if we can make you a bit more comfortable. Then perhaps you'll dream of something pleasant.'

'How right you are, Nurse! *Mens sana in corpore sano*, as the Romans used to say.'

'Sounds rude to me! Suppose we put your bed at a bit of an angle?'

'An angle?'

Nurse Andrews explained, 'I often find that if one raises the head and lowers the foot, patients sleep better.'

'I don't think it would help me.'

'Why not try it?' she suggested. 'All these beds are adjustable. There's a little gadget just underneath the frame.'

Miss Frayle gazed with horror at a wheel just in front of her nose and which was evidently the gadget in question.

'Please don't bother, Nurse.'

The woman became coquettish. 'It's no bother, you silly boy! I'm here to make you happy!'

She was just starting to bend down and look under the bed, when Doctor Morelle caught her hand, and pulled her so that she sat on the bed. He assumed the manner of an amorous patient.

'You can make me happy all right!'

'Now! Now! You mustn't get worked up.'

'I certainly shall — unless you sit there and let me hold your hand.'

Nurse Andrews smiled and patted his hand. 'Poor boy! Feeling lonely?'

Miss Frayle was livid with a jealous fury. The nurse's ankles were just in front of her face. Involuntarily, she put out her hand with her fingers tensed, as if she were going to claw at them.

'I can't tell you what a lonely life mine is,' Dr. Morelle said sorrowfully.

'Not married?'

'No.'

'No girlfriend to make a fuss of you?'

'No. Only a secretary.'

Under the bed, Miss Frayle tensed and listened eagerly.

'I'll bet she's awful.'

Miss Frayle writhed with fury. Slowly she undid her brooch and held it so that she could stab with the pin. She hesitated as Doctor Morelle's voice came again.

'Don't let's talk about her.'

'A pasty-faced podge I'll bet!'

'How did you know?'

'They always are. Regular nightmares.'

'That's what woke me up.' Doctor Morelle continued to amuse himself at Miss Frayle's expense. 'Now you've made me think of her again, I'll never go to sleep.'

'Oh, yes, you will. This'll give you something nice to think about.'

There was the sound of a kiss.

Losing all control, Miss Frayle stabbed viciously at the woman's ankles. But at the crucial moment she moved her feet out of range.

Nurse Andrews rose and began tucking in the sheets. 'Now, will you try and settle?'

Doctor Morelle gazed up at her simulating besotted admiration. 'You're wonderful!'

She smiled and patted his hand, before putting out the bedside lamp.

'See you in the morning!' she murmured as she left the room and closed the door.

Doctor Morelle waited for a few moments, then said quietly. 'All right. You can come out.'

A dishevelled but livid Miss Frayle crawled out from under the bed and stood beside it, shaking with fury.

'Now will you kindly get back to your own room and stay there,' Dr. Morelle said evenly.

'Oh . . . How could you?'

'Could I what?'

'That . . . that horrible painted harpy — '

Doctor Morelle smiled blandly. 'Wouldn't you rather be a painted harpy than a pasty-faced podge?'

Inarticulate with hurt and anger, Miss Frayle rushed to the door and went out.

★ ★ ★

The next morning Doctor Morelle paid a visit to the Therapy Room. All the patients who were having a course of Occupational Therapy were in action. They were all men.

Doctor Morelle cast his eye round the room. He began to move towards the one woman in the room, who was working on the loom.

It was Miss Frayle, and she was in the most hopeless muddle. The Doctor stood watching her as she got deeper and deeper into difficulties, and more and more cat's-cradled with yarn.

She became aware of him watching her, and looked up. Forgetting that they were

163

supposed to be complete strangers, she called out to him:

'Don't stand there staring at me! Can't you see I need help?'

'I've received strict instructions that I must in no circumstances interfere in any other patient's Occupational Therapy work.'

'But Doctor Mor — '

Doctor Morelle flashed a warning look at her and interrupted forcefully, just as Miss Molton approached:

'I daresay the doctor will assist you, madam. I certainly will not.'

'And how are we getting on with our weaving?' Miss Molton asked.

Miss Frayle was close to tears. 'I'm in a terrible tangle.'

'Good gracious, you've got the warp muddled up with the woof.'

She started to extricate Miss Frayle.

'Exactly what I was saying, madam,' Dr. Morelle said dryly. 'Very warped!'

He smiled blandly at Miss Frayle and moved away.

Miss Frayle looked after him vindictively. 'If he hadn't distracted my attention, I'd have been all right,' she muttered.

Leaving the disgruntled Miss Frayle, Doctor Morelle wandered round the room, apparently aimlessly but actually examining the inmates carefully. He approached the French windows, which led onto the terrace outside. He looked out and then concentrated on what he saw.

Approaching along the terrace was the man with the bandaged face.

Doctor Morelle looked round to make sure that he was not being observed, and then went out onto the terrace.

Miss Molton had just completed disentangling Miss Frayle when Cortez and Nurse Andrews came up to them.

'Well, and how did you get on with your weaving?' Cortez asked, smiling coldly.

As Miss Frayle hesitated Miss Molton said brightly: 'Well, we may not be very skilful yet, but we're full of energy.'

'It hasn't hurt your hand?' Cortez asked.

'No, thank you.'

'Then supposing you try the piano?' Nurse Andrews asked slyly.

Miss Frayle became thoroughly alarmed. 'Oh, no, really, thank you. Not yet.'

'I'd like to see whether you find your fingers looser,' Cortez said firmly.

'But it might disturb the other patients,' Miss Frayle said desperately,

'There's no one in the lounge at the moment.' Nurse Andrews said relentlessly.

She and Cortez got on each side of her. And the hapless Miss Frayle had no option but to go with them.

On the terrace, Doctor Morelle had caught up with the man with the bandaged face.

'Good morning,' Doctor Morelle said genially.

'Good morning.'

The Doctor took out his cigarette case. 'Have a cigarette?'

The man pointed to his bandages, ''Fraid I can't.'

'What bad luck,' Doctor Morelle said, taking out a cigarette, then: '*Atishoo! Oh, blast!*' As he sneezed violently, he deliberately dropped the cigarette case. He pulled out his handkerchief as the man bent down to pick up the case and handed it back to him.

'Thank you so much. That was very stupid of me. Ah — ' He sneezed again and in using his handkerchief he contrived to wrap his handkerchief round the case and put it in his pocket.

Meanwhile in the lounge, Miss Frayle, Cortez and the nurse had arrived at the piano. Cortez opened the instrument for her, while Nurse Andrews pulled out the piano stool.

Very reluctantly Miss Frayle sat down on it.

'What are you going to play?' the nurse asked, smiling coldly.

'I . . . I really don't know.'

'Why not run through the programme you gave at your last concert?' Cortez suggested.

Miss Frayle sat motionless at the piano, her hands remaining in her lap. The picture of misery, she turned her head and looked up at the woman. She gave a little shiver as she noted the nurse's hard suspicious expression.

She turned her head and found a similar expression on the man's face. 'Well,' he said grimly, 'we're waiting — ' Cortez broke off abruptly as he overheard the voice of Doctor Morelle from outside the open French windows nearby:

' . . . You know, if you were to push those bandages a bit to one side, you *could* get a cigarette in your mouth all right.'

All three swung round.

Just outside the windows the Doctor was offering a cigarette to the man with the bandaged face.

With exclamations of alarmed annoyance, Cortez and Nurse Andrews dashed out onto the terrace.

Miss Frayle, catching an unmistakable signal from Doctor Morelle as he jerked his head, got up and made a dash for the door.

Cortez and the Nurse hurried up to Doctor Morelle and the man with the bandaged face.

'I told you, you mustn't touch your bandages,' Cortez snapped.

'I'm sorry if I've interfered,' Doctor Morelle said.

'This is a very special case,' Nurse Andrews said severely.

Cortez took hold of the man's arm. 'You'd better come along with me and let me have a look.'

As he led the man off into the house, Nurse Andrews glanced at Doctor Morelle, who was wearing an expression of innocent surprise.

'Professor Cortez is operating on him again at 10 tonight. That's why he's so anxious.' She turned and hurried into the house after the two men.

Doctor Morelle pulled out his handkerchief and the cigarette case, and carefully wrapped the handkerchief all round it. Then he carefully placed it into his pocket. Smiling blandly, he moved off in the opposite direction.

★ ★ ★

Safely back in her bedroom, Miss Frayle sat on the bed reading a note she had found waiting for her. As she read, she frowned with angry astonishment, and her lips silently formed the words as she read it again.

It read:

'Thanks to your asinine incompetence, my investigations have been seriously prejudiced. Kindly refrain from any further interference and stay in your room until you hear from me.'

Miss Frayle crumpled up the note and flung it across the room in the direction of the half-opened window. Jumping up from the bed, she wandered angrily about the room, repeating odd phrases from the note.

' . . . Asinine incompetence, indeed . . . further interference . . . how *dare* he?'

She had wandered to the window. Glancing down, she gave a start as she beheld Doctor Morelle strolling down the drive, away from the house. He was walking somewhat unsteadily, and slowly — like an invalid.

Doctor Morelle reached the end of the drive and turned. Directly he was out of sight of the house he quickened his pace and hurried away.

Back at the house, Miss Frayle had been leaning out of the window looking after the Doctor until he was out of sight. Now she turned back into the room, an expression of profound uncertainty on her face.

Catching sight of the crumpled note on the floor, she bent down to retrieve it. Straightening it out, she read it once more.

Her expression changed to one of determination as she tore the note into very small pieces. Moving to the door, she opened it gently, and peered outside to make sure the coast was clear.

She slipped purposefully outside.

Doctor Morelle had emerged from the lane and came out onto a main road. He began thumbing at passing traffic, and before long a lorry drew up alongside him. He jumped onto the cab.

Meanwhile, Miss Frayle was crossing the hall on her way to the corridor outside the Therapy Room.

Suddenly she caught sight of Cortez and Nurse Andrews approaching. Quickly she managed to slip aside into a nearby recess, and they passed by without noticing her, on their way to Count Otto's study.

Miss Frayle emerged from her concealment and continued on her way.

In Count Otto's office, Cortez and Nurse Andrews were reporting to him. The trio stood at his desk.

Cortez said, 'Nurse Andrews is quite sure this Carnegie woman is a phoney.'

'There's nothing wrong with her hand,' the woman confirmed.

'And I'm certain she can't play the piano,' Cortez added.

'But why should she come here?' Count Otto asked, puzzled.

'That's it. Why? I don't like it,' Cortez said.

'Supposing she's on to something?' the nurse said.

'Oh, no.' Count Otto shook his head. 'She is so stupid.'

'We can't run any risks,' Cortez insisted.

'Of course not, my dear Mark. Please do not worry. If we *should* have any trouble with Miss Carnegie, I have a very good plan for making sure she won't harm us.'

'But — '

'That's all!' Count Otto said sharply. 'Now, let us get down to business.' He turned to sort put various papers on his desk, and all three bent over the desk to examine them. 'What is for today?'

'Tonight, I propose finishing the special job,' Cortez said.

'The face?'

'That's right. Ten o'clock.'

Elsewhere, Miss Frayle was in the ground floor corridor at the spot where she had earlier witnessed Cortez and the Nurse apparently disappearing. She was feeling along the wall for some kind of knob or projection — entirely unsuccessfully.

Giving up, she muttered an exclamation, and petulantly kicked the wainscot with her foot.

She nearly jumped out of her skin as the secret panel slid aside. Immediately she realized that she had discovered how Cortez and Nurse Andrews had disappeared. She went into the opening and closed the panel behind her.

Moving along the narrow corridor Miss Frayle quivered with excitement as she came to a door clearly marked No. 10.

Slowly turning the handle, Miss Frayle cautiously peered inside. The room was empty, so she advanced to the door opening into the Consulting Room.

In Count Otto's study, the white-haired man was putting away the papers he had been discussing with Cortez and Nurse Andrews. 'Very nice! Very good! Then everything is planned.'

'Except one thing,' Cortez demurred.

'What's that?'

'That increase in my share of the dough.'

'Oh, that!' Count Otto spoke carelessly. 'Yes, yes, that we will settle.'

'When?' Cortez asked sharply.

'When you have finished the face. If that is successful, then, of course I agree. You have earned it.'

'But it's successful now,' Nurse Andrews protested. 'Tonight's operation — '

Count Otto gave the woman a sharp glance, his lips tight. 'This is not your business, so please to keep quiet!'

'Come along, nurse,' Cortez soothed, and she followed him to the door.

'And now, where d'you go?' the Count asked.

'To the Operating Theatre. I want nurse to start preparing right away.'

Miss Frayle had been having a good look round in the Consulting Room. Having found nothing startling, she opened the further door and passed into the Operating Theatre.

In the corridor outside, deep in conversation, Cortez and Nurse Andrews stopped at the section of the wall containing the secret panel. The woman was still unconvinced about how far they could trust Count Otto.

'But, Mark, I'm sure he'll try and double-cross you!'

'I can take care of myself.'

'It's this constant putting off. Darling, I feel in my bones it's dangerous to wait.'

Cortez smiled. 'Still worrying about that Carnegie woman? Otto's right. She's too dumb to bother about.'

He pressed the knob with his foot. The panel opened and they went inside.

In the Operating Theatre, Miss Frayle was still looking around. Her eye was caught by a glass-topped table, on which were lying several photographs.

She picked up one and looked at it. Then she picked up another and excitedly compared them.

She recognized one as a picture of Arthur Mason, the same one she had seen in the newspaper. The other one was the same photograph, but with a different-shaped nose sketched in on the photograph — the result being an almost complete change in appearance.

Finding the door to the waiting room open, Cortez frowned and went into the room, Nurse Andrews a short step behind. They halted as they saw that one of the cupboard doors was open.

'Have you been down here?' Cortez asked sharply.

'Not since this morning.'

Cortex strode across to the desk and looked at the papers. 'Someone's been looking through these!' he exclaimed.

'But who can have — ?' Nurse Andrews broke off as a faint noise from the

Operating Theatre reached her ears.

They exchanged warning glances, then moved to the door, gently turning the handle.

In the Operating Theatre, Miss Frayle was hurriedly searching through the rest of the photographs. She selected two more, compared them with the first two. Suddenly she froze as a Cortez's voice spoke behind her.

'You're interested in photography, Miss Carnegie?'

She gasped and spun round. Cortez and Nurse Andrews were standing in the doorway. They were staring at her with grim and unsmiling faces. Then they slowly advanced, every step one of menace.

'May I ask what you are doing here?' Cortez asked harshly.

Miss Frayle stared at him speechlessly for a long moment. Then, finding unsuspected courage:

'I'd like to ask you something first.'

'Well?'

Miss Frayle held out one of the photographs. 'D'you know who this man is?'

'Of course. He is a patient of mine.' Cortez strolled over to an instrument case.

'What's his name?' Miss Frayle asked, her voice tense with anxiety.

Cortez turned to face her, leaning against the case. Nurse Andrews was watching both of them, her expression strained.

'He rejoices in the unromantic name of Higginbottom,' Cortez said blandly.

'Oh no, he doesn't. His name is Mason — Arthur Mason.'

Nurse Andrews moved towards Miss Frayle.

Cortez now had his hands behind his back, deliberately concealed from Miss Frayle as he pulled open a drawer and picked up a hypodermic syringe. 'That's absolute nonsense!' he laughed.

Miss Frayle was now so worked up that she threw caution to the winds.

'That's Mason! And he's a murderer!'

An amused smile crossed his face as Cortez said, 'My dear Miss Carnegie! What an imagination you have!'

He turned his back on Miss Frayle and quickly filled the hypodermic syringe from a small bottle. Miss Frayle was still unaware of his intentions.

'It's not imagination! It's true!'

Nurse Andrews had now reached Miss Frayle and caught her by the arm. 'Now, quiet, please.'

As Cortez approached them, Miss Frayle shook off the nurse's arm.

'I'll not keep quiet! You know it's true just as well as I do. And I believe you're in league with him! You're helping him change his appearance!'

Cortez grabbed her arm.

'That's enough, Miss Carnegie.'

'No, it isn't! I'm going to tell the police! I shall — *Ow*!'

She suddenly broke off and gripped her forearm, as Cortez ruthlessly plunged an injecting needle into her.

'What've you done? Something pricked me! I won't have . . . I won't have . . .'

Her voice trailed away, as she swayed drunkenly, and then passed out completely. Nurse Andrews, prepared for the reaction, caught her as she fell, and laid her down on a low settee. She and Cortez stood looking at her, Cortez playing with the empty syringe.

In the outside corridor, the man with the bandaged face glanced at his watch: *9.50 p.m.* Coming to the wall by the secret panel, he looked up and down the corridor to see he was not observed. Then he bent and pressed the knob and went inside as the panel opened.

Entering the Waiting Room, he looked around him and again checked the time with his watch and the Waiting Room clock.

He picked up a magazine off the table, then settled to wait the few minutes to his scheduled appointment.

He glanced up expectantly as Nurse Andrews came from the Consulting Room. 'I told you I'd be punctual,' he said.

'Good boy! Actually, you'll have to be patient and wait a little.'

'Why? What's up?' Slight anxiety tinged the man's voice.

'Just a rush job. Patient's already in the Theatre. Have you seen Professor Cortez?'

'No. Room was empty when I came down.'

At that moment Cortez came into the

waiting room from the door leading to the stairs.

'Hurry up!' Nurse Andrews said crisply. 'We're all ready in there.'

'No need to panic,' Cortez shrugged. 'I'll be along in a minute. Prepare the anaesthetic, will you? 40% mixture with 1/5 grain adrenol.'

He went through the door leading into the dressing room, closing it behind him.

Nurse Andrews looked at the bandaged man. 'Read your magazine, and relax. We shan't be long.' She turned and went into the Consulting Room.

Miss Frayle was lying strapped onto the operating table. The effect of the knock-out injection had worn off and she had regained full consciousness. Her terrified gaze was fixed on a white-coated and masked figure that was standing by the instrument case and selecting a series of what appeared to Miss Frayle as the most fearsome-looking surgical instruments.

The door from the Consulting Room opened and Nurse Andrews came in. She reported to the surgeon.

'He'll be here in a moment. He's just

putting on his overall and mask.' Going over to a side-table she started to prepare the anaesthetic.

The surgeon moved over to Miss Frayle, towering above her, looking down and twisting a wicked-looking scalpel in his hands.

'What's happening?' Miss Frayle gasped.

'Shall we call it — an abscess, which must be removed?' The surgeon's voice was muffled and distorted by his mask.

'But I'm not in any pain!' Miss Frayle stammered.

'If we were to leave it, you very soon would be.'

In the waiting room, the man with the bandaged face was reading his magazine as the door of the dressing room opened and a figure came out wearing white overalls and his mask, pulling on his rubber gloves.

'Tread on it, Professor. Don't keep me hanging about.'

The figure gestured with his hand but did not speak.

'After all,' the man added, 'I'm head of the queue, really!' Again the figure gestured and then went through the door into the Consulting Room.

In the Operating Theatre, Nurse Andrews was just completing her preparations, whilst the surgeon stood looking at Miss Frayle.

'But you *can't* operate without my permission!' Miss Frayle said desperately.

'I can assure you it's necessary to save your life,' the surgeon said implacably.

The door opened and the anaesthetist came in. He went straight over to the table where Nurse Andrews was working.

'Come along, Cortez!' the surgeon snapped. 'The patient is getting restless!'

Miss Frayle was now becoming frantic. 'I tell you, I won't let you operate! I demand to see Count Otto!'

'He can't help you. That is a surgeon's job.'

'I won't agree! I don't trust you! I demand you see what Count Otto says.'

The surgeon pulled up his mask — to reveal the coldly smiling face of Count Otto himself.

'There! Now you should be satisfied, Miss Carnegie.'

Miss Frayle could only stare at him in

speechless horror as he continued:

'You can rely on me. I have told you the truth. I am operating to save your life. You see, you have interfered where you were not wanted, and, unfortunately for you, have got to know too much. So — I have to deal with you.'

'You're going to murder me!' Miss Frayle whispered, horrified.

'Certainly not!' the Surgeon snapped. 'That would be clumsy, and unnecessarily dangerous. No, just a little operation on the brain, quite easy and straightforward, and when you come to, Miss Carnegie, you'll be a lunatic, just harmlessly insane, and consequently incapable of giving any evidence that might inconvenience me.'

Fear and horror rendered Miss Frayle incapable of making any reply.

'Now, Cortez, are you ready for me to start?'

Nurse Andrews had completed her work, but the anaesthetist was still hesitating. He was looking up at the clock. It was still a minute short of 10 o'clock. Then, clumsily, he spilled the preparation that the nurse handed him.

With a muttered apology, he picked up the fallen tray. A shocked Nurse Andrews stared at him suspiciously.

'What's happening, Nurse?' Count Otto barked.

'He's upset the tray! What is it, Mark?'

Count Otto stared at him for a moment or two, then suddenly reached out his hand and pulled aside his mask, revealing the man to be none other than Doctor Morelle.

Staring across at the revealed face, Miss Frayle's eyes lit up. She suddenly found her voice.

'*Doctor Morelle!*'

'Doctor Morelle!' Count Otto echoed.

'Oh, my God!' Nurse Andrews exclaimed, transfixed.

'Quick! Help me!' Count Otto snarled, flinging himself at Doctor Morelle, who deftly avoided the scalpel, and grappled with the enraged surgeon.

As the struggle continued, Nurse Andrews came to life and joined in. Fighting against the two, Doctor Morelle was almost on the point of being overcome when the door from the

Consulting Room suddenly burst open and an Inspector of Police and two constables rushed into the room.

Doctor Morelle's assailants were quickly overpowered. Count Otto, his face twitching with surprised fury, was held between the two constables, whilst the Inspector firmly held Nurse Andrews.

'Thank you, Inspector,' Doctor Morelle said, breathing hard after his exertions. 'You are commendably punctual.'

'Your telephone message didn't leave me much time but I did my best.'

Doctor Morelle was rapidly regaining his usual composure, along with his breath. 'You've picked up the man with the bandaged face?'

'Yes. My other men outside have got him.'

'Good. He's Arthur Mason the Bank Murderer. By the way, you'll find Professor Cortez where I left him — bound and gagged in the dressing room.'

'Thank you, Dr. Morelle. I expect my men have found him.' He looked at the two constables. 'Let's get this prize pair out of here, and charge them.'

As they left, Doctor Morelle crossed to the operating table, and started to free the excited Miss Frayle. His manner appeared unusually gentle and kind.

'I'm afraid you've had rather an anxious time,' he murmured.

'I knew you'd save me somehow.' Miss Frayle sat up, her eyes shining.

'I won't rub it in, but you would have escaped all this unpleasantness if you'd stayed in your room as I told you.'

'I was afraid you thought I was exaggerating,' Miss Frayle said ruefully, as the Doctor chafed her writs to help restore her circulation.

'It's difficult to exaggerate the criminal organization which Count Otto and Cortez, assisted by the woman Andrews, have built up.'

'Were they friends of Mason's — ?' Miss Frayle broke off at the sound of shouting coming from the Consulting Room, where the Inspector was interviewing the bandaged man, in the company of a couple of policemen.

'I tell you my name isn't Mason! I'm Jim Burdock.'

'We've got your photograph. If that's your story, take off your bandages!'

'You bet I will!' The man tore off his bandages, and glared about him triumphantly.

His nose was completely different from that of the man in the photograph. There was a livid scar down the side of his nose.

'What's that scar?' the Inspector asked.

'It's a burn. That's why I came here.'

The Inspector was visibly taken aback as he looked from photograph to the protester. 'The nose is quite different,' he muttered, than gave a slight start as Doctor Morelle's sardonic voice came from behind his shoulder.

'Of course, Inspector. He's had it changed by plastic surgery.'

'It's a lie!' The man yelled angrily. 'You can't prove I'm Mason.'

Doctor Morelle glanced at the Inspector as he came alongside.

'You checked the fingerprints on the cigarette case I left at the local police station this afternoon?'

'Certainly. They were Arthur Mason's all right.'

'And that's the man who picked it up for me when I dropped it!' Doctor Morelle said, pointing at the scowling Mason.

'That settles it,' the Inspector said decisively. 'Take him away.'

The two policemen removed the struggling Mason from the room.

'This is a real racket that Otto and Cortez have been working here,' the Inspector commented.

Doctor Morelle nodded. 'It'll pay you to go through the other inmates here with a toothcomb. Their Occupational Therapy was nothing but a course of training for cat burglars and the like.'

'A real tough house.' The Inspector glanced sympathetically at Miss Frayle as she joined them. 'If I may say so, Miss, you've had a very lucky escape.'

Miss Frayle smiled and affectionately took Doctor Morelle's arm. 'I knew Doctor Morelle wouldn't let anything happen to me!'

'I must congratulate you, Doctor, on outwitting these crooks so completely,' the Inspector said.

'It needed very little cleverness to cope with a bunch of nitwits who were going to rely for their safety on an operation on something which simply doesn't exist.'

The Inspector and Miss Frayle looked puzzled.

'An operation on something that doesn't exist?' the Inspector asked.

'I refer, of course,' Doctor Morelle said dryly, 'to Miss Frayle's brain.'

Miss Frayle's expression changed from loving admiration to wounded pride.

5

The Cornish Holiday

It was only on very rare occasions that Doctor Morelle could be prevailed upon to take a holiday. He usually took the view that a change of work was sufficient to give a man that mental exhilaration which the majority derive from their usual fortnight at the seaside. And, with his medical work and his delving into matters criminological, he thought that life was sufficiently varied in itself without any need to resort to the artificial stimulus of a holiday by the sea.

Now and then, however, he decided that a change of air would be advantageous, and one fine summer day he and Miss Frayle might have been seen packing a strange assortment of things into a large black instrument case.

'Take particular care of this lens, Miss Frayle,' the Doctor said, handing to her the object in question. 'Pack it, if you can possibly manage to do so, in not too close proximity to the geological hammer which I perceive you have not placed in its cover.'

'Yes, Doctor Morelle,' Miss Frayle said in her most obedient manner.

'It is essential that these instruments are so packed that they do not injure each other,' the doctor went on, explaining almost in the tone that most people would have used towards a not particularly intelligent child.

'Yes, Doctor Morelle.' Curiously enough, the doctor did not appear to find anything particularly suspicious about his secretary's unusual meekness.

'And now the net, please,' the Doctor added, handing this to Miss Frayle in its turn. 'No, no!' he snapped suddenly. 'Not like that; detach it from its steel ring first. Use whatever rudimentary form of intelligence you can command, if you don't find the effort too much for you.'

'I must say,' commented Miss Frayle with a giggle, 'it looks a funny lot of stuff to be taking away with you on a seaside holiday, Doctor.'

'I perceive nothing about it,' the Doctor replied, 'which is calculated to excite a risible reaction. Might I ask what you consider so vastly amusing in a perfectly mundane object like a hammer used in connection with geological excavations?'

'Well . . . ' Miss Frayle hesitated, 'I . . . I'm not at all sure that . . . '

'Or a portable fish net?' pursued Doctor Morelle with relentless logic. 'Or a portable microscope for the study of marine and conchological minutiae?'

Miss Frayle giggled again. 'It couldn't be less funny, Doctor, when you put it like that,' she said.

'Nor,' added Doctor Morelle severely, 'was I aware that our proposed visit to Tintagel was in the nature of a pure vacation, which is usually a lazy man's excuse for being even more lazy than is his normal habit.'

'But you said that we were going there for a change,' Miss Frayle objected, with a pout.

'Did I say so?'

Miss Frayle looked at her employer

with some considerable surprise. 'You certainly did, Doctor,' she remarked, 'And so, naturally enough, I thought . . . '

'That inert nebula which you are pleased to call your mind,' the Doctor said snappishly, 'was promptly directed by a mood of wishful thinking.'

Miss Frayle looked at the Doctor wistfully. 'Then it is not to be a holiday?' she said.

'I shall have considerable work for you to do while we are on the Cornish coast,' Doctor Morelle explained. 'In addition to the various scientific implements which you are now packing on my behalf, you will also require some of your larger and more capacious notebooks, in order to cope with all the necessities of the situation.'

'Oh, dear!' Miss Frayle exclaimed. 'And Tintagel is such a romantic place, too.'

'Indeed?' Doctor Morelle's raised eyebrow suggested an infinite scepticism as to the alleged romantic background that gave rise to such emotions in Miss Frayle.

'It always makes me think of King Arthur's Castle, and those lovely Knights of the Round Table — you know, Lancelot and Queen Guinevere and all those people.'

Doctor Morelle regarded her severely. '*I*,' he said, with a marked emphasis on the pronoun, 'am concerned with the coastal phenomenon of North Cornwall. There I anticipate to discover certain marine manifestations which may or may not be due to the relative proximity of the Gulf Stream to the coast, and on which I propose to write a paper for the *Journal of the Meteorological Society*. The subject is a little outside my own special scientific field, but it is a matter which has been unaccountably neglected by meteorologists, and it well merits the attention of all who wish to study the effect of geographical position on climatic changes.'

'Oh, how thrilling, Doctor!' exclaimed Miss Frayle; but it must be admitted that there was an undercurrent of sarcasm in her voice that somehow escaped the Doctor's usually critical attention.

'I am happy,' Doctor Morelle replied, 'to perceive that the project is now awakening your interest, Miss Frayle.'

'I can hardly wait!' she exclaimed, and still the Doctor apparently failed to perceive that she was not altogether serious.

'Kindly ensure that you have our railway tickets, and confirm that our reservations at the Tintagel Inn are in order,' the Doctor said.

'Yes, Doctor,' Miss Frayle replied with a sigh.

'Incidentally,' the Doctor remarked, 'there is no historical evidence acceptable to the intelligent student which would support the legend of King Arthur and those beings whom you so romantically refer to as the Knights of the Round Table.'

On the long journey down from Waterloo the Doctor was buried deep in a massive tome on some meteorological theme. From time to time he raised his head and endeavoured to persuade Miss Frayle of the foolishness of the author of the book that he was reading. According to the Doctor the man had written the most arrant nonsense on various matters connected with weather science, and he thought that it was high time that the man was shown up as the charlatan that he undoubtedly was. This, and nothing less, was what Doctor Morelle had set himself to do.

Miss Frayle was, of course, not over-impressed by the Doctor's expositions. She was, indeed, only anxious to be allowed to read. Her selection of reading-matter for the journey was, however, not so heavy as the Doctor's. She had brought with her a novel, the colourful cover of which had brought a snort of disgust to the Doctor's face as soon as he caught sight of it.

But when they had settled down at the Inn, and had made their way to the cliff-top, Miss Frayle forgot all about the Doctor's sarcasm on the subject of her selected reading.

'Oh, Doctor!' she exclaimed, flinging her arms wide and drinking in the air. 'Isn't this really heavenly?'

The Doctor sniffed the air and looked around him with interest. 'The visibility is indeed indicative of fine weather tomorrow,' he said.

Miss Frayle looked thoughtful. 'What you said about King Arthur and his Knights being all nonsense may be right, of course, Doctor,' she remarked.

'It is indubitably right, my dear Miss Frayle,' the Doctor replied, somewhat mollified to perceive that Miss Frayle had indeed taken in what he had said just before they had left London.

'Still,' she went on, 'when I look out to sea with those lovely rocks down there below, I'm sure it could have been true.'

'I am only sorry, Miss Frayle, that you have no real sense of scientific meaning of historical evidence,' the Doctor replied in his most severe tones.

'I feel just like a bird up here,' Miss Frayle went on with a sigh of pleasure, 'Oh, for the wings of a gull!' She stood up and moved forward two or three paces.

Doctor Morelle smiled sardonically. 'You will certainly need wings in a minute, Miss Frayle,' he exclaimed, 'if you don't come away from the edge of the cliff. You are rapidly approaching a spot which seems to be more than ordinarily dangerous for the careless pedestrian.'

'What an unromantic person you are, Doctor!' Miss Frayle exclaimed. She sighed again. Then she pointed down below them: 'Look, Doctor! There's someone swimming down there.'

'I have already perceived him,' Doctor Morelle said. 'He appears to be making for the shore. If we wait we shall observe the precise position of the path by which he will no doubt ascend the cliff to the spot — more or less — on which we are now standing.'

'That's a good idea,' said Miss Frayle brightly, continuing to watch the swimmer down below them.

Doctor Morelle chuckled his rather mordant chuckle. 'I have been known to have good ideas on occasion, you know, my dear Miss Frayle,' he said.

'And after that shall we go down to the beach?' Miss Frayle asked eagerly.

'I think not,' the Doctor replied.

'Oh.' There was infinite disappointment in Miss Frayle's voice.

'We will note where the path runs,' the Doctor explained patiently. 'Then we will make our return to the Inn without further unnecessary delay.'

There was no doubt at all that Miss Frayle was deeply disappointed. She was one of those people who like to do things as soon as thought of, and who feel irritated and annoyed by having to put anything off for a later occasion.

'I'd like to have gone down now,' she said.

'We will go tomorrow morning,' said the Doctor.

'Tomorrow?'

'Yes, I have arranged for the hire of a rowing-boat with a capable oarsman in charge. It will be awaiting us on the beach tomorrow.'

Miss Frayle clapped her hands with glee. 'A rowing-boat,' she said. 'How lovely.'

'I have arranged that it will be awaiting us on the beach at six a.m.,' the Doctor explained.

'Six in the morning!' exclaimed Miss Frayle in horrified tones.

'Yes.' The Doctor seemed unable to understand Miss Frayle's dislike of early rising.

'By why at that unearthly hour?' she asked.

The Doctor smiled. 'It will enable us to get in few hours' work before breakfast,' he said.

'I should think it will,' Miss Frayle commented. Then she said: 'Oh, well, I suppose that it's good for us. Here's that swimmer coming up the cliff path now.' She regarded the man with interest. 'Oh, yes!' she exclaimed as the man came in sight.

'Might I enquire what is the precise meaning of that inane monosyllable?' the Doctor said.

'I recognise him,' Miss Frayle explained.

'Yes?'

'His name is Sutton,' said Miss Frayle. 'He's staying at the Inn, you know.'

Doctor Morelle looked somewhat surprised at this revelation of the stranger's identity. 'You appear to have made the gentleman's acquaintance with considerable rapidity,' he said. 'We have scarcely been here for two hours as yet.'

Miss Frayle smiled. 'I always like to know who's who and what's what right away,' she said. 'There are only two other guests at the Inn besides ourselves.'

'Indeed?' Doctor Morelle managed to inject into that one word a suggestion of infinite sarcasm.

'Mr. Sutton and Miss Bell,' Miss Frayle went on. 'They are related, as a matter of fact. I think she said that they were cousins. She had been very ill, you know. Mr. Sutton is her solicitor as well as being her cousin.'

Doctor Morelle again smiled his most sarcastic smile. 'Miss Bell,' he said quietly, 'obviously has considerably garrulous tendencies.'

'How clever of you to know that, Doctor,' replied Miss Frayle, 'when you have never met her! Yes, she does run on rather when once she starts talking.'

By this time the swimmer was approaching them. 'Good evening, Mr. Sutton,' said Miss Frayle as he approached.

He was rather breathless after making the ascent of the steep cliff. 'Good evening,' he said. 'And it's a marvellous evening, too. I've just been in for a dip. Often go in the evenings, as a matter of fact. In some respects it is the best part of the day for anyone who takes swimming at all seriously.'

'I observe,' said Doctor Morelle quietly and seriously, 'that you have some considerable aquatic prowess.'

'Eh?' Sutton said, apparently puzzled by this tribute. Then it seemed as if he suddenly realised what was the meaning of the Doctor's comment. 'Yes,' he said. 'I used to do quite a lot of swimming at one time. Won quite a few pots and things. You're staying at the Inn, aren't you?'

'Yes,' said Miss Frayle, unable to resist engaging this friendly stranger in conversation. 'I've already met your cousin, Miss Bell. I'm Miss Frayle, and this is Doctor Morelle.'

'How do you do?' said Sutton. Doctor Morelle bowed in silence, and looked out to sea.

'Is the bathing quite safe here?' Miss Frayle asked, her mind clearly fixed on the costume that, unknown to the Doctor, she had decided to bring with her, even if the stay in Cornwall was not to be regarded entirely as a holiday.

'Oh, yes, I think so,' Sutton replied. But there appeared to be a suspicion of doubt in his voice, a suggestion of not being quite sure whether he had given the correct reply.

Even Miss Frayle, not usually very sensitive to the nuances of tone, realised that there was some little doubt as to the meaning of Sutton's reply.

'I suppose a strong swimmer like you doesn't have to worry, anyhow,' she said.

'It's safe enough for anybody,' Sutton said seriously, 'so long as they manage to keep somewhere fairly near to the shore. It's only some distance out that the currents get at all dangerous, you see.'

Miss Frayle chuckled. 'I always try to keep one foot on the bottom, anyway,' she said.

Sutton laughed. 'Well, I must run on, if you'll excuse me,' he said. 'Can't risk a serious chill by hanging about, you know. I'll see you anon.'

He moved towards the Inn, and Miss Frayle looked at the Doctor. 'I suppose we'd better be getting back, hadn't we, Doctor Morelle?' she said. 'After all, we shall have to be getting up at the crack of dawn, shan't we?'

Doctor Morelle smiled his humourless smile. 'Your somewhat highly coloured description scarcely fits the hour of six a.m., my dear Miss Frayle,' he said. 'However, we are to have something to eat before retiring, and I presume that it would be as well if we soon make our way back to the Inn.'

Miss Frayle certainly went early to bed. She knew that it would be difficult enough to get up by six the next morning, and she had no desire to merit the rebuke which would undoubtedly be her portion if she overslept and kept Doctor Morelle waiting at a time when he desired to start work. For his part the Doctor sat up well after midnight in his room, still studying the book on meteorology that had so occupied his attention on the journey down from Waterloo that morning. But it seemed as the Doctor, like so many intellectual folk did not need more than a minute ration of sleep in order to keep going.

The next morning they were at the

beach at six o'clock, but the boatman did not turn up. Doctor Morelle perceived the boat that he had hired, and so, with Miss Frayle, he decided that they could go out without the attendance of the boatman.

Miss Frayle, who fancied herself a little as an oarswoman, took the oars, while the Doctor, armed with a net, proceeded to attempt to gather some specimens of the local flora and fauna, which he seemed to think would give us some valuable pointers as to the influence of the Gulf Stream on the climate of that part of the coast.

Miss Frayle, indeed, was a powerful if not very effective oarswoman.

'It is not necessary for you to pull at the oars with such vigour, Miss Frayle,' said the Doctor, when they had got some distance from the shore. 'It will be quite sufficient for the moment if we allow ourselves to drift with the tide.'

Miss Frayle shivered. 'I'm only trying to keep myself warm, Doctor,' she said. 'I find it very cold as early in the morning as this, you know.'

'Nonsense!' the Doctor exclaimed. 'There is but the lightest of breezes, and the sun is shining.'

'It may be shining,' Miss Frayle said with another shiver, 'but there's no warmth in it as early as this.'

Doctor Morelle looked at her sternly. 'Kindly allow the boat to drift, as I requested, Miss Frayle,' he said. 'My net has become entangled in weed — species of chorda filum, I fancy. Quite an interesting specimen of hydrophyte.'

Miss Frayle obediently stopped rowing, and the boat drifted slowly. The Doctor drew in his net slowly and regarded carefully the dull-looking seaweed that was entangled in it.

'Madly interesting, Doctor!' Miss Frayle commented with as near an imitation of the Doctor's savage sarcasm as she ever allowed herself to approach.

'What's that?' she exclaimed after a moment.

'Help! Help!' came a woman's voice from the near distance.

'Good gracious!' Miss Frayle said. 'What on earth is that, Doctor?'

'A cry for assistance,' Doctor Morelle said. 'Quickly, the oars, Miss Frayle! Move aside and let me take them.'

'Oh, dear,' Miss Frayle grumbled, moving with extreme caution, to ensure that she should not upset the boat, something which she was terrified she might do if she did not move with the greatest possible care. Doctor Morelle, on the other hand, moved quickly but with considerable skill.

'Help! I'm drowning! Help!' came the woman's voice from the distance.

Doctor Morelle was already rowing with that air of quiet efficiency that marked everything that he did. Miss Frayle looked around her helplessly. It was on such occasions that she felt herself completely at a loss to know what best to do.

'Sounds as if it's somewhere around the other side of that rock, Doctor!' she said. 'Hurry, do!'

'My dear Miss Frayle,' Doctor Morelle said. 'You might observe that I am rowing as hard as I can. I trust that we shall be there in time.'

And, indeed, the woman's voice was coming closer and closer as they rowed. They could now hear the actual words she was speaking far more distinctly than they had previously been able to do.

'Richard!' she was screaming. 'Richard, where are you? Help me — I'm going . . . ' Her voice faded away on a note of despair, as if she was quite unable even to hope for assistance any longer.

'There she is — ' Miss Frayle exclaimed, gesticulating wildly. Her eyes opened wide. 'I believe it's Miss Bell!'

'Are you sure of the lady's precise identity, Miss Frayle?' asked the Doctor, still rowing hard and not looking up as he spoke.

'I'm almost sure,' she said. 'Oh!'

'What is the reason for that exclamation?' Doctor Morelle asked quietly.

'She's gone under, and there is Mr. Sutton over there,' Miss Frayle exclaimed.

'Mr. Sutton!' she shouted, and their acquaintance was swimming around and around, as if in search of someone.

Doctor Morelle seemed to ignore his secretary's attempt to attract the attention of the man. 'Are you approximately in the region in which the lady sank, Miss Frayle?' he asked suddenly.

'Yes, yes!' Miss Frayle agreed excitedly.

Doctor Morelle carefully removed his coat. 'Take the oars now, quickly,' he warned Miss Frayle.

'I've got them.' Miss Frayle said. For once, indeed, she was quicker in action than Doctor Morelle had been able to anticipate in his thoughts.

'I hope we are in the right vicinity,' Doctor Morelle said, showing, practically for the first time in their joint career, a real sense of anxiety.

'I'm sure we are,' Miss Frayle said. 'In fact, I think that I can see her down there.'

'Good,' Doctor Morelle commented. 'And when I dive, keep the bows steady, if you can.'

'Dive?' Miss Frayle repeated in some consternation. 'But, Doctor . . . ' It seemed she was intensely puzzled by the way in which the Doctor was now taking complete control of a very difficult situation.

'I glimpsed something beneath the surface of the water then,' Doctor Morelle said. 'Keep the boat quite steady, Miss Frayle, if you can possibly manage to do so.'

And without more ado the Doctor stepped over the edge of the boat, into the water.

'Oh, Doctor Morelle!' exclaimed Miss Frayle, her hand over her mouth. 'Can you swim?' She paused for a moment and watched him. Then she murmured to herself: 'I suppose he can; he's gone under.'

Then she started suddenly. Another voice addressed her. It was Sutton, who had swum towards them, and was now hanging on to the edge of the boat. 'Does the Doctor know just where she went?' he asked breathlessly.

'Yes, Mr. Sutton,' Miss Frayle exclaimed. 'He's caught a glimpse of her under the water, and I think that he'll manage to get her out.'

'Wait,' puffed Sutton. 'Wait until I get my breath. Then I'll give a hand. I've been swimming around . . . and around. I feel quite breathless, you see.'

Miss Frayle had been watching the spot where Doctor Morelle had gone under the surface.

'Doctor Morelle!' she exclaimed suddenly.

'What is it, Miss Frayle?' asked Sutton excitedly.

'I believe he has got her!' Miss Frayle was now full of delight at the way in which the Doctor had succeeded.

Doctor Morelle was now on the surface, supporting the woman by her armpits, and treading water successfully.

'Swing the boat over, Miss Frayle,' he said, in no way alarmed at the experience that he had undergone.

Miss Frayle had to summon to her aid all the scanty knowledge of rowing which she possessed in order to bring the boat into the position that the Doctor desired. She succeeded, however, in getting to the side of Doctor Morelle and the other woman.

'Lean over the stern and lift her under the arms,' the Doctor ordered.

Miss Frayle did as requested, and in a moment she managed to get a satisfactory grip of Miss Bell.

'I've got her, Doctor,' she said.

'Hold her steady. Don't try to move her in any way. Just hold her until I get aboard,' Doctor Morelle said.

As the Doctor scrambled into the boat Miss Frayle felt her grip slipping. 'Help me, Mr. Sutton,' she said.

'Yes, yes, I'm here, Miss Frayle,' Sutton gasped, still breathless, but managing to get around. Before he could do anything to assist, Doctor Morelle, dripping and looking almost comic in his wet clothes, clambered into the boat.

'All right, I've got her,' the Doctor said, taking over from Miss Frayle, and pulling the inert body of Miss Bell into the boat in an apparently effortless fashion.

'Thank heavens you turned up,' Sutton said.

'Get in the boat, Mr. Sutton,' Doctor Morelle snapped. 'You'd better take one oar. Miss Frayle, you take the other.'

'Yes, Doctor Morelle,' Miss Frayle said obediently. Many times in the course of her career she had felt an intense admiration for the Doctor, and for his capacity to face a critical situation, but never, she thought, had he seemed to her so admirable as now.

'I'll try artificial respiration,' the Doctor said. 'We must try to get her ashore as soon as possible.'

In a few short minutes, indeed, the whole situation was altered. Miss Bell had been taken to her bedroom, and Doctor Morelle was attending to her. Miss Frayle and Mr. Sutton had adjourned to the bar, where they each sipped at a brandy — a stimulant that the situation somehow seemed to demand.

The landlord looked at them sympathetically. 'What a dreadful thing to happen,' he said.

'Yes,' Miss Frayle agreed.

'Poor lady,' sympathised the landlord, shaking his head from side to side.

'Terrible, terrible,' said Sutton.

'Please try to calm yourself, Mr. Sutton,' Miss Frayle said. 'Doctor Morelle is with her now, you know, and if anyone can save her, I can assure you that he will.'

The landlord grinned. 'I just been down to the office and 'phoned for a proper doctor,' he announced at length.

Miss Frayle was intensely irritated by this. 'What do you think Doctor Morelle is?' she asked, 'a Doctor of Music?'

The landlord was not impressed by this. 'What I can't understand, Mr. Sutton,' he said, 'is how a strong swimmer like yourself didn't manage to get to Miss Bell afore she sank.'

'I know,' said Sutton, 'That's the awful part of it, you see.'

'What exactly happened, Mr. Sutton?' asked Miss Frayle in some curiosity, as always impelled, in the absence of Doctor Morelle, to ask what she regarded as leading questions.

'Well,' said Sutton, and then hesitated. 'You see, Miss Bell has often swam out as far as that with me before. And this time, when I turned round to make for the shore, she was a bit behind me.'

'Yes?' Miss Frayle had for the nonce adopted the technique which she had often observed in Doctor Morelle — the technique of getting the witness to tell the story in the words which seemed to him most suitable, and with the absolute minimum of interruptions.

'I didn't hear her call to me,' Sutton went on, 'and I was half-way back before I heard her first shout for help. Of course, I turned back at once, but I couldn't see her!'

'Couldn't see her?' repeated Miss Frayle in incredulous tones.

'The sun in my eyes dazzled me,' Sutton explained. 'When you are swimming, with your eyes close to the water, it's almost impossible to see anything if you are really in a straight line with the sun, and it is shining right in your eyes.'

'Of course,' Miss Frayle agreed.

'I had to try and judge where she was by the cries she was uttering,' Sutton went on. 'That's why it took me so long to reach you. You will remember, I'm sure, Miss Frayle, that when you saw me first I was nowhere near her.'

Miss Frayle started, and then suddenly turned back towards the door. With her infallible instinct she had realised that someone was coming into the room.

'I'm sure,' said the Doctor's familiar voice, 'that you will all be very relieved to learn that . . . '

'Oh, Doctor Morelle!' Miss Frayle exclaimed, startled in spite of herself. 'You made me jump!'

Sutton looked at him, with an expression very difficult to read at the back of his eyes.

'Mr. Sutton,' Doctor Morelle broke in.

'Doctor,' Sutton said. 'Have you got any news for me?'

'News?' Doctor Morelle asked.

'Yes, news. News of my cousin.'

Doctor Morelle's face creased into what was doubtless intended to be a reassuring smile, though, with his normal expression of sarcasm, it was not at all easy to understand it as such.

'You will doubtless be considerably relieved to learn that she has recovered,' the Doctor said.

'Miss Bell's alive?' the landlord of the Tintagel Inn exclaimed in incredulous tones.

'Precisely,' Doctor Morelle said in his usual suave manner. He had changed his soaking clothes, and now he was at last himself again.

'So you see that your telephone call for

what you describe as a proper doctor was totally unnecessary.'

Miss Frayle's eyes opened very wide indeed. 'Why, Doctor,' she said, 'I do believe that you have been eavesdropping on our conversation!'

Doctor Morelle disregarded this interruption. It seemed that, as usual, he considered Miss Frayle's remarks beneath his contempt.

'On the other hand,' he went on, still addressing the landlord, 'it would be very appropriate if you had made another call.'

'Another call, Doctor?' The landlord was clearly completely mystified by the turn that the conversation was taking, and he made no effort to hide his mystification.

'Yes,' answered Doctor Morelle.

'Another call to who?' asked the landlord.

'To the police,' answered Doctor Morelle in his most dramatic tones. Miss Frayle looked at him in amazement. She was, indeed, just as surprised as the others by the turn of events.

'Police?' the landlord echoed.

'Yes.'

'But what's wrong?' asked Sutton.

'Your story of how you failed to save your unfortunate cousin from drowning!' answered Doctor Morelle.

'Doctor!' exclaimed Miss Frayle.

'What . . . what . . . what on earth do you mean, Doctor?' stammered Sutton, his face a study of puzzlement.

'I mean that it was a deliberate attempt on your part to murder her,' the Doctor explained.

Miss Frayle afterwards said that she was always destined to remember the events of the next few minutes. There was such a complete pandemonium in the place, with Doctor Morelle grappling with Sutton, who seemed suddenly to have taken leave of his senses. Then, when he had been overpowered by Doctor Morelle, not unaided, it must be admitted, by his swordstick, the landlord was directed to 'phone the police.

The whole course of events was so sudden and so swift that Miss Frayle was forced to admit that she was completely unable to appreciate what was going on.

It was only when they were installed in their comfortable sitting room in the Tintagel Inn that she was able to request the Doctor to explain what had happened, and the way in which he had spotted what was going on.

'Quite apart,' he said, 'from the fact that, since he was taken into custody, I have learned that Sutton embezzled a considerable sum of money from Miss Bell — money entrusted to him by her — it was made quite obvious to me that her narrow escape from drowning was in no way an accident.'

Miss Frayle, as always on these occasions, was duly impressed. She was driven to confess that she was completely mystified by the fact that the Doctor had spotted the error made by the would-be murderer.

'I must say, Doctor,' she said, 'I can't for the life of me think of a reason why you should, for a moment, have suspected that he wanted to murder Miss Bell.'

'You amaze me, my dear Miss Frayle,'

the Doctor said, 'I should have thought that the whole affair was abundantly obvious to anyone with an analytical brain.'

'Thank goodness,' Miss Frayle said, 'that I have some sort of effect on you sometime, Doctor.'

'The guilty person's detailed description of what had taken place, my dear Miss Frayle,' the Doctor went on sententiously, 'was quite clearly a complete fabrication from beginning to end.'

'You mean about the way in which he swam off to the shore, heard Miss Bell call for help, turned back, and was not able to see her?' Miss Frayle inquired.

Doctor Morelle smiled sardonically, 'Because the sun dazzled his eyes?' he said.

'Yes, Doctor.'

'Precisely,' the Doctor said. 'It was in that very point that Sutton went so completely astray in his attempt to deceive us as to what had occurred.'

'I'm afraid that I don't follow you, Doctor,' Miss Frayle admitted sadly.

'My dear Miss Frayle,' the Doctor said

slowly, 'may I be permitted to acquaint you with a perfectly simple geographical fact, which I should have thought was well within your comprehension, even with your limited mental capabilities?'

'You may, Doctor Morelle,' Miss Frayle said, for once ignoring the insult.

'At this precise moment, we are on the north coast of Cornwall,' the Doctor said. 'I may, I hope, take it that you will not wish to dispute that fact?'

'You may, Doctor.'

'When we look out to sea we are therefore facing due West,' the Doctor pursued. Miss Frayle nodded.

'And that would therefore be Sutton's position when he turned back from the shore in the direction of his drowning cousin,' explained Doctor Morelle.

'Yes,' Miss Frayle agreed, but it appeared that she still did not appreciate what Doctor Morelle was trying to prove.

'Yet,' went on the Doctor, 'he declared that the sun was in his eyes, and that it dazzled him. The sun which rises in the East, and, at that time in the morning, would be directly behind him!'

The light of comprehension came into Miss Frayle's eyes. 'Good gracious me, of course!' she exclaimed. 'Oh dear, when will I ever think of the right solution to these problems?'

Doctor Morelle smiled again. 'On that breathless occasion,' he said, 'the sun will rise in the west, and, no doubt, there will simultaneously be a blue moon swimming in space above!'

6

The Bodyguard

There are few cases of Doctor Morelle that can be related in full without Miss Frayle coming very much to the forefront of the picture. Indeed, some of the Doctor's most eminent friends have been known to say that Miss Frayle was in some respects the most important part of the Doctor's criminological equipment, though the lady — and certainly Doctor Morelle himself — would probably have indignantly denied any such suggestion.

But their adventure at Tintagel had brought on a definite chill in Miss Frayle, and the Doctor, reluctantly enough, had been compelled to request her to stay in Cornwall for a few days longer, while he, many professional engagements in prospect, had to come back to London.

For the first day or two he seemed completely lost; he had become so accustomed to Miss Frayle's methods that even her mild inefficiencies, which almost drove him crazy, now seemed enviable in retrospect. Before the end of a week it became obvious that he would have to find a temporary secretary; to carry on without one was completely hopeless. The Doctor lost papers and forgot important appointments, on occasion he wrote scientific papers and sent them, untyped, to the wrong journals. In fact, the whole thing was so hopeless that he even welcomed the rather hearty young woman who was sent around to him by an employment agency, although she tended to annoy him as much by her heartiness as Miss Frayle had done by her quietness and apparent mental density.

It was on the third morning of the regime of Miss Wentworth (for that was the name of the temporary secretary) that the 'phone rang with that compelling urgency which phones seem to have on occasion. Miss Wentworth took up the receiver with an air of brisk efficiency.

'Doctor Morelle's house,' she said.

The voice at the other end of the

telephone sounded extremely puzzled. 'Oh,' it said — it was a man's voice. 'Er . . . that's not Miss Frayle, is it?'

Miss Wentworth smiled. 'No,' she said, 'I am Miss Wentworth, temporary secretary to Doctor Morelle. I'm afraid that Miss Frayle is still in Cornwall. She went down there with the Doctor, caught a nasty chill, and so she hasn't been able to come back yet. I understand that there is every chance that she will be back within a matter of a week or ten days.'

'I'm sorry to hear that,' said the man at the other end. 'Is the Doctor away too?'

'Oh, no,' Miss Wentworth replied. 'He left Miss Frayle in Cornwall and came back to town. He is here.'

'Good,' replied the man on the 'phone. 'Well, my name is Carson and my wife is a patient of the Doctor's.'

'I see,' Miss Wentworth said. 'Will you please hold on for a few moments? The Doctor's in the laboratory, and I'll go and tell him, if you'll wait.'

'Thank you,' said Carson. 'I'll hold on with pleasure if you can get him.'

Miss Wentworth made a mild grimace

at the telephone, as she laid the receiver quietly down and made her way to the laboratory. It was an indication of the healthy respect that the Doctor had instilled into his temporary secretary that she knocked gently on the laboratory door, and waited until she heard his 'Come in,' before she ventured to enter. As soon as she had opened the door and made her way into the laboratory the Doctor, seated at a desk and surrounded by papers, snapped: 'What is it now, Miss Wentworth?' He sounded more than usually irritable, but that did not worry Miss Wentworth.

'A Mr. Carson is on the 'phone, Doctor,' she said. 'Wants to speak to you at once, he says.'

Doctor Morelle glared with unconcealed annoyance. 'Is the matter important?' he asked.

'He didn't say,' Miss Wentworth explained cheerfully.

'Well, it is a great nuisance,' added the Doctor, 'as I am now busily engaged in collating these notes on the case of the paranoid poisoner of Paris.'

Miss Wentworth shuddered delight-edly. 'I see,' she remarked, 'that sounds rather a gruesome business, doesn't it, Doctor?'

'It is not intended to be an account of a vicarage fete,' the Doctor snapped. 'I think that I asked you whether Mr. Carson's business showed any signs of being genuinely important, Miss Wentworth. Do you think that you could possibly give me an answer to that question?'

'Well, really,' Miss Wentworth replied. 'I'm afraid that I didn't ask him if the matter was really important. He said that it was about his wife, who had been a patient of yours.'

'Very well,' said Doctor Morelle, and then looked very thoughtful for a moment. 'Miss Frayle hasn't telephoned from Cornwall yet?' he added.

'No, Doctor,' replied Miss Wentworth.

'I just thought that she might be ringing up at any moment,' explained the Doctor. 'In any event, I am expecting her to do so sometime today. Kindly inform me as soon as her call comes through — and meanwhile I will take Mr.

Carson's call in here. You can switch it over from the other instrument outside, if you would be so kind.'

Miss Wentworth stood by in silence. Doctor Morelle looked at her with some surprise.

'That's all,' he said. 'You can go now, Miss Wentworth.'

'Oh . . . er . . . yes, Doctor,' she replied slowly. 'I was just looking.'

The Doctor followed the direction of her eyes. She was looking in an almost fascinated way at a shelf above his head.

'You were looking, Miss Wentworth?' he said.

'Yes; is that a real skull up there?' she asked. 'I say, that's a bit gruesome company, isn't it?'

Doctor Morelle had been irritated before. Now he was positively savage, and he fairly glared at Miss Wentworth.

'On the contrary,' he said. 'I almost invariably prefer a human skull for company to a human being. Would you kindly *go*?'

'Oh, yes Doctor,' she said, at last surprised into acquiescence with his wishes. She made her way to the door and left the Doctor alone. After she had gone, he muttered between his teeth: 'And I never thought it possible that anyone could be more stupid than Miss Frayle!'

He slowly made his way across the room to the telephone, which stood on a bench at the other side of the laboratory.

'Hello,' he said, removing the receiver and raising it. 'Doctor Morelle speaking.'

'Good morning, Doctor,' said Carson's moderately familiar voice at the other end. 'It's Carson here. It's my wife. I'm really a bit worried about her, and I thought that I could do with your advice in the matter.'

Doctor Morelle drew a scribbling pad silently towards him and took up a pencil. 'Tell me as briefly as you can what is giving you cause for concern,' he said.

Carson paused. 'Well,' he said, 'you know that she had that irrational fear that her life was in danger.'

'Yes, yes, you need not remind me about the past history of a patient,' Doctor Morelle said. 'I naturally retain a detailed memory of what was wrong with a patient whom I have been treating as recently as in the case of Mrs. Carson.'

'Well, she still has the fear that her life's in danger,' Carson explained, 'And that she may be robbed of her jewellery.'

Doctor Morelle snapped: 'I have already explained to you her illness is in the nature of an anxiety complex — a perfectly simple psychological condition which every psychiatrist has had to deal with fairly frequently.'

'Yes, yes, that's true, Doctor,' Carson said. 'And I'm glad to say that, thanks to your treatment, she was getting very much better. The trouble is that I have to go down to our factory at Kidderminster — we're working out a new programme of production of some special types of carpet to assist the export drive, you see.'

'But I don't understand exactly what is the point of these remarks,' Doctor Morelle said.

Carson hastened to explain. 'I shall be away at least a fortnight, you see, Doctor,' he said.

Doctor Morelle scribbled a few notes on the pad that was close to his right hand. 'Doubtless,' he remarked, 'your proposed absence for such a comparatively long time is largely responsible for the return of the imaginary fears which caused so much trouble in the past.'

'You think so?' Carson said.

'I am sure,' the Doctor replied. 'I am not in the habit, Mr. Carson, of making unsupported suggestions unless the facts warrant me. I will call on you before midday to advise on treatment which will be appropriate for the situation which has arisen.'

'Thanks very much,' Carson said. 'I'm sure that a visit from you will make all the difference to her condition. I will expect you about twelve o'clock, shall I?'

Doctor Morelle usually found himself able to bury himself completely in whatever work he had in hand. An appointment for midday would, as a rule, in no way disturb his equilibrium during the morning. But on this occasion he found his mind moving from the criminological case on which he was working, and on to the medical case which was so soon to hold his attention.

Mrs. Carson had, indeed, been in many ways a sad case; but she was in no way unusual, since she presented a matter that had so often previously been dealt with by Doctor Morelle in the course of his psychological experience. He was, indeed, more than a little surprised that any kind of recurrence of the trouble had come, for in his lengthy experience the treatment which he had suggested was practically invariably successful. A relapse, such as apparently set in with Mrs. Carson was so rare as to be surprising. The Doctor found himself thinking back to this point, thus being totally unable, as has been said, to concentrate on the affair in hand.

By eleven o'clock the Doctor was extremely worried. By half-past eleven he thought that it was high time he set out for Mr. Carson's house, near to Hyde Park.

He was received by a butler who, with proper ceremony, asked him to wait in the lounge whilst he fetched Mr. Carson.

Doctor Morelle, who was not quite his usual self, said quietly: 'While I am waiting I would like to make a telephone call, if I might do so.'

'Certainly, sir,' the butler replied. 'They is a 'phone here, you see.'

'I had already perceived that,' Doctor Morelle replied with something like his normally caustic manner.

'Would you like me to get the number for you, sir?' the butler asked.

'Thank you,' Doctor Morelle said. 'It is my own house that I want — ' He gave the number.

The butler dialled it, listened for a few moments, and then handed the receiver to Doctor Morelle, with a 'You're through, now, Doctor.'

Doctor Morelle spoke into the receiver: 'Doctor Morelle here,' he said.

Miss Wentworth, in her usual hearty voice, said: 'No, I'm afraid that he is out at the moment. This is his temporary secretary, Miss Wentworth.'

'It *is* Doctor Morelle speaking,' the Doctor said in irritated tones.

'No, he isn't in,' Miss Wentworth replied blandly. 'Can I take a message for him, please? I will let him know about it the moment he comes back.'

Doctor Morelle took a deep breath. 'Will you kindly cease your prattle, Miss Wentworth?' he snapped. 'I am Doctor Morelle trying — if only you will allow me to do so — to speak to you and to give you a message.'

'Oh!' Miss Wentworth said in surprised tones, 'You *are* Doctor Morelle? I'm so sorry, Doctor — I thought that it was someone asking for you. Can I help you?'

Doctor Morelle grinned his humourless grin. 'That probability seems doubtful in the extreme!' he exclaimed. 'However, if you could by some miracle manage to bring your attention to bear upon what I have for the past few minutes been unsuccessfully trying to say to you . . . '

'Go ahead, Doctor,' Miss Wentworth replied cheerfully, 'I'm all ears!'

Doctor Morelle thought that this was a remark best left without comment. 'Miss Frayle has not yet telephoned from Cornwall, has she?' he asked.

'Not yet; no,' Miss Wentworth replied.

'Should her call come through while I am here,' the Doctor went on, 'and she appears to you to be in any way anxious to speak to me urgently, will you tell her that she can get me at this number — Park 86000.'

'Park 36000,' Miss Wentworth said.

'86000,' the Doctor corrected her.

'Okay,' replied Miss Wentworth. 'I will give her your message if she rings up.'

The Doctor replaced the receiver with a slam. He was finding Miss Wentworth more and more trying as time marched on; but he did not see that there was very much that he could do about it, as he knew that she was supposed to be the best that the employment agency could supply.

As he turned from the telephone he saw Carson approaching.

'Ah, there you are, Doctor Morelle,' Carson said, holding out his hand in a friendly fashion.

'I failed to hear your approach,' the Doctor said quietly.

'Sorry if I startled you,' replied Carson with a cheerful smile.

'My nerves are invariably completely under control,' the Doctor rasped.

'This carpet's pretty thick,' elaborated

Carson. 'Got it all over the house. My wife's idea; she likes quiet. By the way,' he added in sympathetic tones, 'I was sorry to hear about Miss Frayle.'

'Merely a slight chill,' Doctor Morelle said. 'Contracted through her own fool-hardiness, naturally. Nothing serious at all. In fact, she is much more anxious about me than I am about her. She is, in many ways an odd young woman, I'm afraid. She has a curious complex that she is quite indispensable to me in my work. Nothing could be further from the truth, of course.'

'Ah!' murmured Carson. 'I always say that no one is indispensable, no matter who they are.'

'With one or two exceptions, just to prove the rule, of course,' Doctor Morelle remarked, with pointed emphasis. 'And about your wife, Mr. Carson? If it is at all possible, I should like to see her without delay.'

'She is in her room, Doctor,' explained Carson.

'And how does she appear?' enquired Doctor Morelle.

'As a matter of fact,' Carson confided, 'I haven't seen her myself this morning yet. As you know, she had been sleeping very badly, so as a rule she isn't awakened before midday if it can possibly be avoided.'

'I see,' said the Doctor.

Carson paused. Then he went on: 'By the way, I didn't mention that I've had a sort of bodyguard here the last few days. He's all right, and, as these fears of hers grew worse, she insisted on having someone of the sort with her. So, just to pacify her, I arranged for this chap to come in.'

Doctor Morelle looked more than a little annoyed at this revelation of what had been done in the household.

'The fundamental basis of the treatment which I prescribed is to imbue the patient with a feeling of self-confidence,' he said in annoyed tones.

'I realised that, of course, Doctor,' Carson admitted.

'And to allay her fears by external means might easily ruin the effect of the treatment which I have been putting forward,' the Doctor said. 'Who is this person whom you have engaged for the post which you described, I think, as being that of a bodyguard for your wife?'

'Chap recommended to me by a friend of mine,' said Carson, 'He is a tough-looking fellow, all right. He sort of patrols the garden outside my wife's window, and sometimes the corridor outside her room.'

Doctor Morelle sniffed sarcastically. 'The arrangement,' he said 'appears to be somewhat unusual, not to say dangerous. If you will be so kind as to conduct me to your wife as soon as she is ready, Mr. Carson . . .'

The butler suddenly burst into the room. His face was contorted in alarm. 'Mr. Carson!' he exclaimed. 'Sir!'

Carson looked at the manservant with an expression of agitation and excitement. 'What is the matter?' he asked. 'What has happened, Rawlings?'

'It's . . . it's . . . it's Mrs. Carson,' gasped the man.

'Mrs. Carson? What has happened to her?' asked Carson, his face growing suddenly pale.

'She's been attacked by someone!' explained Rawlings, still gasping with the strain and excitement of the message that he was bringing.

'What on earth d'you mean?' asked Carson.

'Please come, sir,' pleaded Rawlings. 'She's unconscious, and I didn't know what to do about it.'

Carson looked almost irritated by the manservant's insistence.

'All right, all right, we're coming,' he snapped, 'Calm yourself, man! I think that you had better come along too, Doctor. It looks as if you might be wanted, from what Rawlings says about my wife. Let's hurry.'

They made their way swiftly into the bedroom, where Doctor Morelle, taking command of the situation in his usual alert manner, examined the prone, apparently lifeless figure on the bed.

Carson stood by, quite still. It seemed that this had come as a complete surprise to him, and he was in no way prepared for what had happened.

'This is a ghastly business, Doctor,' he

said in subdued tones — almost a whisper.

Doctor Morelle looked up from his examination. 'Very regrettable.' He agreed dryly. 'Your wife, however, will undoubtedly make a successful recovery.'

'Thank heavens for that,' Carson said, with a sigh of relief. 'Obviously, I should think, she was awakened by the thief, who attacked her and, as is obvious, got away with her jewellery.'

Doctor Morelle nodded gravely, his eyes still fixed on the patient. 'You would appear, Mr. Carson, to have formed a correct picture of what occurred.'

The door opened, and a tall man with a tanned face entered.

'Er — ' he began, and then stopped suddenly and looked at Doctor Morelle. Then he turned back to Carson, and said, slowly, 'Mr. Carson.'

'Come in Hamilton,' Carson said. Then he added to Doctor Morelle: 'This is the chap I was speaking to you about, Doctor.'

'The . . . ah . . . bodyguard,' Doctor Morelle said quietly.

'Yes,' said Carson, adding in bitter tones: 'Though he seems to have been in some way off his guard at the moment when his work might have been useful.'

Hamilton looked as if he thought that this was an extremely doubtful compliment. 'I'm very sorry, sir,' he said, though his voice did not seem to indicate any real contrition. 'Dreadful business, it us, I'm afraid. The thief must have done it just as I was off duty for forty winks.'

'What time would that be?' This question, suddenly snapped out by Doctor Morelle, seemed to catch Hamilton completely off his guard.

There was a quite perceptible pause before the man replied, sullenly: 'About half-past three this morning, I should think it was.'

'And you didn't hear anything at all suspicious?' his master asked, a tone of quite definite suspicion in his own tone as be spoke.

Hamilton was very hesitant in his reply. 'Well, sir,' he said, 'as a matter of fact, I did. But, you see, I thought that it was the butler.'

Carson frowned. 'When was this?' he asked,

Hamilton apparently thought that a lengthy explanation was now necessary. 'Well, sir, you know that my room is three doors away from Mrs. Carson's,' he began.

'Yes, yes,' said Carson impatiently. 'You can take it that we know all about that, Hamilton. Cut out all the unnecessary stuff, and get down to telling us exactly what it was that you heard in the night.'

'I was just dozing off,' Hamilton explained, 'when I thought that I could hear footsteps outside, in the corridor. Sort of quiet, creepy footsteps, they were.'

'What did you do?' asked Carson.

'I slipped out of bed,' Hamilton explained, 'opened my door quietly, and saw the butler.'

'Where was he?' snapped Doctor Morelle, watching the man's face very closely as he replied.

'He came out of the room and hurried away.'

'He was coming out of my wife's room?' asked Carson in tones of the most complete incredulity.

'That's right,' Hamilton confirmed.

'And you didn't hear anything from my wife?' enquired Carson.

'No. The butler was in his stockinged feet, you see,' said Hamilton.

'Why did you not see fit to make any report of this highly suspicious occurrence at an earlier hour?' asked Doctor Morelle pointedly.

'I thought of doing so,' Hamilton admitted. 'But you see, Mr. Carson, I know that your butler was an old servant, and so I decided that it was probably only that Mrs. Carson had sent for him to help with something.'

'All right, Hamilton,' Carson said. 'You'd better tell him that I should like to have a chat with him right away.'

'Very good, sir,' Hamilton said. 'I'll see if I can find him, and then I'll send him in to you.'

When Hamilton had left the room Carson looked at Doctor Morelle his face expressive of complete amazement and bewilderment.

'What on earth do you make of that

story, Doctor Morelle?' he asked.

'I'd prefer to offer no suggestion at the moment, Mr. Carson,' the Doctor said. 'I never like to generalise on insufficient data, you see. Let us await the butler's arrival in as much patience as we can command.'

In a moment the butler arrived. 'You wanted me, Mr. Carson?' he said.

'Yes,' Carson snapped. 'Can you tell me where you were at about half past three this morning?'

It was now the butler's turn to look bewildered. 'In bed, of course, sir,' he said.

'Sure?'

'Quite sure, sir.'

Doctor Morelle looked at the butler with the same intense gaze that he had formerly given to Hamilton. 'You are quite certain about that?' he said.

'Quite certain, as I have already assured Mr. Carson, sir,' he said, emphatically.

'Then how,' asked Carson, stabbing the air with a admonitory finger, 'do you account for the fact that Hamilton saw you coming out of Mrs. Carson's room at that time this morning?'

The butler looked both amazed and indignant at the same time.

'Hamilton says that?' he said.

'Yes.'

'I tell you,' he said, 'that I was fast asleep at half-past three this morning.'

'H'm.' Carson did not seem to be very impressed by this denial.

'And if Hamilton said that he saw me anywhere outside my room at that time, he must have been dreaming!' added the butler with more emphasis than ever. Indeed, his voice now sounded quite angry at the suggestion that had been made.

'No need to get excited,' Carson said, 'I'm only asking you, you know.'

Doctor Morelle now again took a hand in the questioning. 'You are sure that *you* were not dreaming?' he said. 'After all, some people have been known to indulge in somnambulism — walking in their sleep.'

'I don't know what on earth you're getting at,' the butler said. 'It seems to me that Hamilton has been trying to cast suspicion at me over this business.' He looked at Carson, a glance of appeal in his eyes. 'Mr. Carson, sir,' he said, 'I've served you faithfully for many years. You know that I wouldn't touch your wife's jewellery if it was the last thing . . . '

'Quite, quite,' agreed Carson soothingly. 'Is there anything more that you'd like to ask him, Doctor?'

'Nothing more,' Doctor Morelle said quietly, as if he was sure that he now had all the necessary information within his own possession, and required no more questioning, in order to fill in gaps of knowledge.

'Right,' Carson said to the butler. 'You can go away.'

'Very good, sir,' said the butler, walking slowly from the room. It was obvious that the course of events had considerably shaken him.

When the door had shut behind him Carson turned to Doctor Morelle. 'Well, this is a queer business, Doctor Morelle, and no mistake,' he said.

'On the contrary,' Doctor Morelle said dogmatically, 'the case appears to me to be in every possible way perfectly straightforward and simple to deal with.'

'How do you mean?' asked Carson in bewilderment.

'I have a theory, which has often been proved, that every criminal makes a mistake, and that anyone who is sufficiently alert can invariably spot what is the mistake, thus being led to the culprit inevitably.'

'I cannot believe it!' said Carson incredulously.

'This case, in fact, furnishes yet another example of the person concerned committing a glaring flaw, which reveals him as the undoubted culprit.'

'I find it difficult to believe that you have worked the whole thing out like that,' asserted Carson. 'After all, I have heard all the cross-examination which you have conducted. And yet I cannot say that I have the least idea of who it is. I can't believe that a man I have employed for years can possibly be a criminal, and yet . . . and yet . . .'

Doctor Morelle waved all this aside with an imperious gesture.

'From the start, of course,' he said, 'the man Hamilton — your so-called body-guard, employed to safeguard your wife and her habits — revealed himself to me as the criminal. He gave himself away inevitably to me when he described the manner in which he heard what he thought were suspicious footsteps outside your wife's room three doors away from his own.'

Carson frowned. 'There seemed to be nothing wrong with that as far as I could see,' he objected.

'One aspect of your residence,' Doctor Morelle went on, apparently changing the subject in an arbitrary manner, 'strikes me as being apparent to the eye, and yet at the same time being somewhat unusual.'

'What do you mean?' Carson asked.

'Your carpets are extremely thick, and they are fitted throughout the house,' Doctor Morelle said.

'That's right,' agreed Carson, still very puzzling at the course that the conversation was taking.

'You will, perhaps, also recall that

Hamilton declared he was about to doze off when he heard further footsteps outside your wife's room — three doors away from his own room! Furthermore, he stated that he identified your butler in the very act of leaving that room, in his stockinged feet. Obviously, it would be totally impossible for him to hear such footsteps in a thick carpet from the position described. Therefore, I assert, he is undoubtedly the criminal.'

'That's brilliant, Doctor,' asserted Carson in admiration.

'He was clearly making a stupid attempt to divert suspicion from himself to your butler,' the Doctor said, 'And yet, had I not been here, he might well have got away with it.'

'And what would you suggest that I should do?' Carson asked, ignoring the suggestion in the Doctor's last remark.

'Ring Scotland Yard, and ask for some senior official,' the Doctor suggested. 'Mention that I have suggested that you should get into communication with them, and tell them what has happened. Meanwhile, do everything you can to lure

Hamilton into a state of false security, so that he will not try to get rid of the jewels before the arrival of Scotland Yard. I am sure that he has then hidden in some safe spot.'

'I don't know how to thank you, Doctor,' replied Carson in tones of the deepest gratitude.

'Don't trouble to do so,' the Doctor said. 'But in future show your gratitude, my dear sir, by trying to carry out my advice. Had you not introduced this bodyguard into the household, this would never have occurred.'

At the moment when Doctor Morelle was proffering this advice, the telephone rang.

'That may be a call for me,' Doctor Morelle said. 'I was expecting a telephone call from Cornwall, as Miss Frayle had expressed her intention of giving me a ring sometime today.'

'Hello?' said Carson, lifting the receiver.

'Is that Mr. Carson?' asked the voice at the other end.

'Yes.'

'I have a call from Tintagel for you,'

said the operator, 'Hold on a minute, please.'

Carson handed the receiver to Doctor Morelle. 'This will be Miss Frayle all right.'

'Go ahead, Tintagel,' said the operator's voice. 'You will have to speak up. The line is not good.'

Doctor Morelle pressed the receiver to his ear. It was true enough that the line was not good. There was a buzzing, crackling noise at the other end, which made it very difficult for him to hear Miss Frayle's voice.

'Is that you, Miss Frayle?' he asked, 'Speak up please, I am totally unable to hear what you are saying. What did you say? What?' He paused, and Carson was unable to repress a smile at the look of surprise and disgust that came over the Doctor's face at whatever it was that Miss Frayle was saying at the other end of the line.

'Speak up, speak up!' the Doctor said in extremely irritated tones. 'You are *what*? But I must forbid you to do anything of the sort!'

Again there was a pause, while the buzzes and crackles from the other end drowned Miss Frayle's voice. 'Remaining in Cornwall to take up a post *there?*' the Doctor said. 'Want to be quiet? How dare you?'

The Doctor's face was now a study. Indignation and surprise fought for mastery in his expression. Never had Carson seen him so baffled and annoyed.

'How utterly and absolutely selfish of you, Miss Frayle!' he snarled. 'No thought for me at all! Here am I with a fool of a woman who can't even take a telephone call properly, not to mention deal with technical dictation!'

Now Carson could hear the murmur of a female voice at the other end of the line. Clearly Miss Frayle was putting her feet down good and proper.

'You know,' resumed the Doctor, now almost pleading, 'that I *cannot* find anyone to take your place ... I must insist on your returning to London without any more delay and taking up your old position immediately. I *command* you!' This was said with such an imperious air that once more it brought a smile to Carson's lips.

Soon, however, the Doctor was more pleading than ever. Now all the old sarcasm seemed to have disappeared from his voice. Now he was clearly desperate with anxiety. 'I . . . I . . . Miss Frayle,' he said, 'I *beg* you to come back . . . But, my *dear* Miss Frayle . . . '

Doctor Morelle jiggled the receiver up and down, hoping against hope that there would be some response. But he was too late. The instrument had gone dead.

THE END

We do hope that you have enjoyed reading this large print book.

Did you know that all of our titles are available for purchase?

We publish a wide range of high quality large print books including:
Romances, Mysteries, Classics
General Fiction
Non Fiction and Westerns

Special interest titles available in large print are:
The Little Oxford Dictionary
Music Book, Song Book
Hymn Book, Service Book

Also available from us courtesy of Oxford University Press:
Young Readers' Dictionary
(large print edition)
Young Readers' Thesaurus
(large print edition)

For further information or a free brochure, please contact us at:
Ulverscroft Large Print Books Ltd.,
The Green, Bradgate Road, Anstey,
Leicester, LE7 7FU, England.
Tel: (00 44) **0116 236 4325**
Fax: (00 44) **0116 234 0205**

Other titles in the
Linford Mystery Library:

F.B.I. SPECIAL AGENT

Gordon Landsborough

Cheyenne Charlie, Native American law student turned G-Man, is one of the Bureau's top agents. The New York office sends for him to investigate a sinister criminal gang called the Blond Boys. Their getaway cars somehow disappear in well-lit streets; they jam police radios; and now they've begun to add brutal murder to their daring robberies. Cheyenne follows a tangled trail that leads him to a desperate fight to the death in the beautiful scenery of the Catskill Mountains . . .

RED CENTRE

Frederick Nolan

Moscow, 1986. The Chief Intelligence Directorate of the Soviet General Staff is preparing to launch the Death Bird, an ultra-secret assault satellite. A pre-emptive measure to ensure the West could never place in orbit any satellite deemed inimical to Soviet interests . . . And in the technological world of espionage, treachery, betrayal and sudden death, only British secret agent David Caine and the lovely Cuban-America widow Lynda Sanchez can prevent the master spy from achieving his ends . . .

THE WALL

E. C. Tubb

Business associates Kerron, Chang and Forrest, three of the richest men on Earth, are old and approaching the end of their days. Desperate to prolong their lives, they seek the man who seems to have the secret of immortality: the mysterious Brett, an adventurer who has apparently lived for centuries. But Brett hides a dark secret . . . and for him to help them, they must accompany him on the most dangerous journey — to the centre of the Galaxy — beyond the Wall!